Witch

Emma Fischel

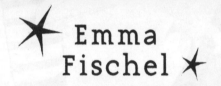

nosy crow

Grandma

Mum

Ghoul

Forest Pixie

8-Year-old
Giant

Troll

First published 2014 by Nosy Crow Ltd
The Crow's Nest, 10a Lant Street
London SE1 1QR
www.nosycrow.com

ISBN: 978 0 85763 417 7

Nosy Crow and associated logos are trademarks
and/or registered trademarks of Nosy Crow Ltd

Text © Emma Fischel 2014
Cover and inside illustrations © Chris Riddell 2014

A CIP catalogue record for this book is available from the British Library.

Printed and bound in the UK by Clays Ltd, St Ives Plc.
Typeset by Tiger Media Ltd, Bishops Stortford, Hertfordshire

Papers used by Nosy Crow are made from wood grown in
sustainable forests.

1 3 5 7 9 8 6 4 2

www.nosycrow.com

For the three little
witchkids at number **17**.
You know who you are…

X

A NOTE
TO ALL
WITCHKIDS

My grandma is eighty-three – and you know what she uses to do spells? A wand. A real old-style wand.

I know. I know. She's probably the only witch in the whole of Witchworld who still does. It's a long black thing, and she has to wave it about and say magic words – lots of them – to make it work. And it's much bigger and slower than a spellstick. But Grandma will NOT be parted from it.

Mum bought her a top-of-the-range spellstick – touchscreen, lime green and with extra-big graphics because Grandma's eyes aren't that good. But Grandma just snorted and turned it into a toad.

Which is what Grandma's like. Stubborn and grumpy and rude.

Also bossy. VERY bossy. It was Grandma who bossed me into writing this book. Grandma said I should tell you my story. She said witchkids need to know about ghouls.

And Grandma is right. You witchkids do need to know about ghouls. Need to know the signs to watch out for. Need to know, if you spot even a hint of a ghoul, to act – FAST.

So here it is. The book that Grandma bossed me into writing. A book about the ghoul attack in Haggspit. Written by a witchkid who was there, part of it, from the very start.

I've tried to be truthful. I've tried to tell it exactly how it was. I hope you find the book useful.

And remember, witchkids. Stay alert. At all times stay alert. . .

VERY alert.

Florence Skritchett

Part
One

Chapter 1

GRATED DRAGON'S TOOTH

DRIED TROLL TOE-NAILS

I'm Florence Skritchett – known as Flo – and I live in Haggspit, the capital of South Witchenland.

My house is in Upper Haggspit, near the top of Moaning Mountain. It's a cave-style house, wide and low and light, and all on one floor. And it's big, because Mum makes lots of money.

Not long ago I lived there with just Mum and Hetty, my sister. But one morning, that all changed...

That morning – Saturday – started like Saturdays usually do.

I was in the kitchen, alone, eating my breakfast.

Then I heard wailing from the other side of the house, which meant Hetty was awake.

Because Hetty does the same thing most mornings. Wakes up, looks in the mirror – and starts wailing.

I heard her feet stomp out of her bedroom and along the corridor, then – *Bam!* – the kitchen door burst open and in Hetty stomped. "Flo, I hate my nose," she wailed. "It's too small. Too neat. Not even one bump! It's just not witchy enough."

Then she flung herself on to a breakfast bar stool and smoke started pouring out of her ears, like it always does when she's upset.

Oh. The nose. . .

Hetty has just finished her witchsits, and she's almost sixteen – and you know what she wants for her birthday?

A nose job potion.

I had to say something, so I did. Because I do love my sister – well, most of the time – but she can be extremely shallow.

"Hetty," I said. "There are only ninety-five forest pixies left in the whole of Witchworld – and what are you worrying about? Your nose."

Hetty ignored me, like she nearly always does when I talk about forest pixies. She just grabbed my arm. "Flo, what can I do?" she wailed. "I'll never

EVER get a boyfriend. Not with a nose like this!"

Just then Mum came sweeping into the kitchen.

Now, maybe your mum would say something sensible. Something like, "Don't worry, Hetty. Witchy noses come in lots of shapes and sizes." Or, "You're still growing, Hetty. There's plenty of time for your nose to sprout lovely big bumps." Or even, "Hetty, a nice witchboy won't care about your nose, he'll care about your character."

I do NOT have a mum like that. More's the pity.

"Darling," Mum said. "I've found you the perfect nose." Then she waved this week's copy of *Hocus Pocus* at Hetty.

Hocus Pocus. The weekly magazine – top seller, although I have no idea why. It's got no actual important news at all. It's just gossip and scandal and pictures of famous witchscreen stars on holiday, with arrows added on, pointing at their wobbling bits.

And I'm sorry to say, my mum is boss of it.

Now Mum was leaning over Hetty and pointing at a picture of a pouty sort of witch wearing skintight robes – very short – with a lot of cut-out bits, posing on the green carpet. "Zoe Shreek," it said underneath. "Star of *Premonition*."

I took a look. Whoever Zoe Shreek was, she had

an extremely witchy nose, long and pointy, and with three bony bumps.

Then Mum patted Hetty on the head. "Not long to wait," she said kindly, because — as I'm sure you know — it's illegal to buy a nose job potion for anyone under sixteen. "Then we'll sort that sad little nose of yours out."

Which is about as mumsy as Mum gets.

And soon after that, Mum swept Hetty out of the kitchen to get ready. They were off shopping for witchwear, because Hetty's school Prom is in one week's time — which means when Hetty's not wailing about her nose, she's wailing about having nothing to wear to her Prom.

I think there's a witchboy who's going that she likes...

Good luck to him, that's all I can say.

The kitchen stretches along one side of my house. It's got curved walls, and curved doors off it. One wall is all windows, floor to ceiling, with big views out. So, sitting at the kitchen table — which I was — I could see across the garden and down the mountain to Haggspit Harbour, way way below.

I could see something else too.

What looked like a tiny black bird, bobbing and

weaving along Skyway 121, making its way up Moaning Mountain.

Except as it got closer and bigger, I realised it wasn't a bird. It was a witch. An old witch. Riding a broomstick, an actual old-style broomstick...

An old witch dressed in long robes, black as black, like something out of my witchhistory book...

An old witch wearing a big pointy hat with stars on it...

It could only be one old witch.

Grandma.

Chapter 2

GRATED DRAGON'S TOOTH

DRIED TROLL TOENAILS

Grandma and her broomstick came lurching up the garden, so I opened the back door and Grandma swooped in. She rammed her broomstick at the floor – which is how Grandma always lands – and hopped off.

"Hello, Flo," she said, giving me a big smacking kiss.

Then things started arriving behind Grandma. Things lurching through the back door and crashing on to the floor – lots and lots of them.

Bulgy old bags, battered pots and pans, a big crate stuffed full of spell books and a whole set of cauldrons – five at least – all stacked one inside another, big to small.

I know, I *know*. No one uses cauldrons any more. But try telling that to Grandma.

All the banging and clattering brought Mum swirling back into the kitchen to see what the noise was. She took one look at Grandma, another look at the big heap of Grandma's stuff piled up in the middle of the kitchen floor – and her mouth dropped right open.

"Mother," said Mum faintly, grabbing hold of a worktop for support. "Are you coming to visit?"

"Not exactly, Kristabel," said Grandma, giving Mum a shifty sort of look.

Guess what? Grandma is homeless – and it's all her own fault.

Grandma lives on the other side of Haggspit Harbour. In a flat in a small block, full of old witches and with a twenty-four-hour caretaker. She's been there for the last five years.

Not any more.

Grandma's been thrown out.

Mum called up the caretaker to find out what was going on – and I could hear him yelling into Mum's skychatter about Grandma. About how she was not allowed back. Ever.

Because the caretaker has had witchmums and witchdads queueing round the block to complain to him about Grandma. About her giving their little witchkids nightmares. About little witchkids waking up screaming and yelling. Refusing to leave the house. Refusing to go to school. All because of Grandma.

It turns out that Grandma has been standing outside local schools and playgrounds, handing out booklets.

About ghouls.

Yes. *Ghouls*.

On the front of Grandma's booklet was a drawing of a ghoul. Dribbling and grinning and evil-looking. Plus this, in big jaggedy lettering:

WITCHCHILDREN!
STAY ALERT!
DANGER OF GHOUL ATTACK!

I started flicking through. Got glimpses of Grandma's vital ghoul information – a diagram of ghoul teeth with an arrow pointing to the fatal biters. Step-by-step self-defence moves in case of ghoul attack. A height chart: ghouls at the top, goblins at the bottom. A map showing where Grandma reckoned ghouls might be lurking…

Oh dear.

Mum was not happy with Grandma. In fact, Mum was very unhappy.

She snatched the booklet off me. "Mother," she hissed. "How could you be so stupid? Ghouls are extinct. Eradicated in the Great Ghoul War!"

"Extinct?" Grandma snorted. "Ghouls are not extinct. And, Kristabel, I have proof they're around Haggspit. I—"

"*Not! Listening!*" screeched Mum, sticking her fingers in her ears.

"Well, you *should* listen," said Grandma, eyes popping indignantly. "Ghouls are underground on Moaning Mountain, somewhere in the Forest of Fears. Digging their way to the surface right now!"

Then Grandma hung her head and kicked at the floor. "And you'll have to take me in, Kristabel," she said grumpily. "I have nowhere else to go — except the gutter."

"I am sure the gutter will be quite comfortable!" Mum shrieked, and swirled off out of the kitchen, slamming the door.

✶

Mum calmed down, of course, and it didn't take long. Because for all Mum's faults — and believe me,

she has plenty – she does love Grandma. Well …
deep, deep down.

She came back in, grabbed an ice pack out of
the witchchiller and pressed it on her forehead. "All
right, Mother," she said. "You can stay but only –
ONLY – until I find you another place."

Grandma gave Mum a high-five, which I taught
Grandma last visit – to keep her busy. Because if
Grandma's not busy she gets bored. And if Grandma
gets bored, she's quite likely to give me antlers, or
turn me purple.

Which is – of course – against the law. But
Grandma doesn't take much notice of laws.

"I'll be NO trouble," Grandma said, beaming.
"You'll hardly know I'm here."

"You *will* be trouble, Mother," said Mum wearily.
"You're *always* trouble."

Mum was right.

Chapter 3

Mum had a talk to Grandma before she and Hetty went shopping.

"While we are out, Mother," said Mum severely, "here are the rules. No leaving the house, no breaking any laws, no involving Flo in anything strange or peculiar – and no talk of ghouls."

"Oh, I promise, Kristabel," said Grandma. "Cross my heart."

She lied.

The moment Mum and Hetty had gone, Grandma got her wand out. "Flo," she said with a glint in her eye. "We have work to do. And no time to lose!"

I backed off. I did NOT like the look of that glint. Or that wand.

"Grandma," I said nervously. "Is this something to do with ghouls? Because Mum said—"

Grandma ignored me. She started waving her wand about, making big looping shapes in the air.

"Abrakkida Dikkit, Telepitti Rottik," she said. And her voice was all strange and singsong, like it always is when she says magic words. "Kronkellikka, Gotikka, Rune." Then she gave her wand one final wave — and pointed it straight at me.

A sprinkle of stardust — shiny and glittering — came shooting out of the end, straight across the room and started whizzing around me.

I felt hot. I felt odd. And most of all, my feet felt itchy. Then they lifted off the floor.

"Grandma!" I yelled. "No!"

But it was too late. I was helpless. My whole body shot itself across the room and on to the back of Grandma's broomstick.

Grandma hopped on the front with a cackle. "We're off!" she said — and we *were off*. Out of the back door and down the garden. Then up, and left…

On to Skyway 121.

Yes — I can hear you all gasping, and I'm not surprised. Grandma knows perfectly well that witchkids are *not* allowed on broomsticks. She knows it's travel by skyriders only for us under-sixteens.

Did it stop her? No.

I clung on. "Grandma," I yelled. "You are BREAKING THE LAW. You'll get arrested the moment a witchwarden sees me on the back!"

"Good point," Grandma cackled. And she turned round, did some more wand-waving, more magic words – and I went invisible.

"Take me home," I yelled. "Now!"

But Grandma ignored me.

So I clung on, invisible and panicking. Because you know how you feel all comfy in a skyrider? All safe in your padded seat, all strapped in and with the flexipod pulled over you, so you can see out but not fall out? And your grown-up in front, driving safely and carefully?

Being on the back of Grandma's broomstick was NOT like that.

It was wobbly, it was uncomfortable and so cold my teeth started chattering. And I didn't like being invisible, not one bit.

Then it got worse.

Because Skyway 121, which is small and almost empty, was bad enough. But then Grandma stuck her arm out and swerved.

Oh no. Grandma was turning left.

"No, Grandma," I shouted. "Not Skyway 1. NO!"

But did Grandma listen? Well – what do you think?

If you've ever flown on Skyway 1, you'll know why I was shouting at Grandma. It's always busy, and it was today. Three lanes, packed solid with skyriders. All sorts – skyscudders, skyshredders, skysnipers, even a forty-seat skyswaggerer with tinted flexipod – all racing along at top speed.

And Grandma, on her broomstick. Lurching along. Weaving from lane to lane without checking. Singing old witchy songs – loud and out of tune.

I could hear horns honking and witches screeching. I had no idea where we were going or how long we would be. I just clung on tight and waited for it to be over.

On and on we flew. Past signs to Kroke, and to Klink, and to Dreem. Past the forests round Ryke. Past the Singing Stillwaters. Past the towers and turrets of Hovelhagg Palace.

"Grandma!" I yelled. "Where are we going?"

"North," Grandma yelled back.

Which was NOT a useful answer.

All of a sudden Grandma swooped sideways off

Skyway 1, towards Gormwitt.

Was that where we were going? Gormwitt? Fourth city of South Witchenland? Famed for its kronkel-milk cheeses?

No.

We weren't.

We were flying lower now. Down and down and down, on a tiny deserted skyway. Past a gritterback, grazing quietly in a field. Two heads down, munching on big grassy clumps. One head up, keeping watch…

That was the head that spotted us.

One look and the gritterback was gone – streaking across the field and into the forest, panicking.

Well, *I* was panicking too.

Because right up ahead of us was a waterfall. A huge waterfall. A vast flowing sheet of water, plunging down into a river. Loud and noisy, thundering in my ears.

And Grandma was heading straight for it.

I shut my eyes. What was she *doing?* "Grandma!" I yelled. "You're going to crash us!"

But Grandma didn't.

She swooped straight through the waterfall – so fast I hardly got a drop on me – swooped through a huge cave, swooped into a tunnel leading off it. A dark tunnel, cold and smelly and very very long.

Then we were out. Swooping and swerving through trees, lots and lots of trees. Zigzagging on and on and on.

Until, at last, we were in a small clearing – and Grandma lurched to a halt.

It was nothing like a skyrider landing. Not smooth and gradual. No. Grandma – as usual – just rammed her broomstick at the ground. Which meant I fell straight off.

I lay on the ground, grinding my invisible teeth and rubbing my invisible knee, which was hurting.

Then Grandma stood over me and waved her wand. "Abrakkida Reditikka," she said, and – slowly, slowly – I started to see myself returning. Along with a big lumpy bruise forming just above my sock.

"How about that for a bit of fun?" Grandma cackled.

I gaped at her. "Fun?" I said. "Grandma, that was irresponsible. And dangerous. And illegal."

But Grandma just snorted. "Witch Wellbeing and Safety," she said. "Bunch of sissies. All those rules. Witchkids as young as three rode on broomsticks in my day. Did they fall off on landing? No. Not after the first time – and nor will you."

Not after the first time?

"Grandma," I said. "There will NOT be a second time."

Then I got out my skychatter. "I'm ordering a skycab," I said. Because Mum has a skycab account and she lets me use it when she's too busy to take me places. "I am going home. Safely. And without breaking any laws."

But Grandma just started waving her wand. "Abrakkida Meskit, Komiskki Kebbula," she said, quick as she could. "Kantorik, Oruskki, Almari, Pardune."

And even though I put in all the right numbers, I got through to the information desk of the Upper Haggspit Junior Choir.

"Grandma," I said, feeling my teeth grinding again. "You had better have a *very* good reason for kidnapping me. Whatever we are here for, it had better be worth it."

"Oh, it is," said Grandma. "It is."

Her eyes gleamed. "We, Flo are in search of a very rare creature indeed…"

Which was when I heard something.

Voices. Little ones. High-pitched. Chattering. Shrieking. Shouting. Arguing. Voices I knew.

Forest pixies.

Chapter 4

Now – I am the number-one fan of forest pixies. I have the following forest pixie items:

forest pixie backpack
forest pixie badge
forest pixie hairband
forest pixie socks
forest pixie key ring
forest pixie skychatter case
forest pixie lunchbox
forest pixie water bottle
forest pixie spellstick holder

```
forest pixie secret journal
forest pixie snow globe
forest pixie toothbrush
forest pixie bubble bath
forest pixie duvet and pillowcase set
forest pixie pyjamas
forest pixie slippers
```

Lots of witchgirls in my class prefer fairies – but I don't. Because we had a big flutter of garden fairies hatch last spring, and I watched them closely, and I discovered this…

The average number of times a garden fairy admires her own reflection in a dewdrop is *twenty-seven* times in thirty minutes.

Dull, dull, dull.

Besides, fairies don't need help. There's billions of them, but not even a hundred forest pixies. Which is why I am also a Friend of Forest Pixies – known as a Frixie – membership number 431782.

If you're not a Frixie, well, you should be. Because forest pixies have no forest. Not any more. Not since Freefall Forest burned down.

Freefall Forest is the only forest in Witchworld with pixies in it – but also the only forest with a ready-potions building on its edge. One where ready-potions for witches get tested on dragons.

Not all witches think it's fair to test ready-potions on dragons. And two years ago, one July night, some of those witches crept into the testing building and set all the dragons free.

The dragons headed straight for Freefall Forest – but dragons and forests are NOT a good mix...

The dragons burned the forest down, every single tree.

So that was it for forest pixies. No homes left. And not many pixies. Ninety-four, to be exact.

That's when the Friends of Forest Pixies started up. The Frixies did lots of fundraising and they replanted new trees in Freefall Forest – but Freefall Forest trees are slow growers. Even watered every day with super-speedy growth potion, it'll take ten to fifteen years before the pixies can use them.

So the Frixies built the Sanctuary. It's half a mile square and in a top-secret location. It's got a strong netting roof and strong netting walls to stop pelloligans getting in and snacking on their favourite food. Which is pixies.

The Sanctuary is as much like Freefall Forest as the Frixies can afford. It's got two fake Freefall Forest trees. Good fakes – well, the pixies seem happy with them. Tall fakes, about as high as a two-storey building, with fake den holes all over the trunk and plenty of fake branches.

There's a special coating on the trunk, so pixies can climb. The first coating was too slippery and the pixies kept falling off. The second coating made the pixies itchy and grumpy. The third coating, the Frixies got it right.

There's other stuff there too. Mud for rolling in, a pond – because pixies are lightning-fast swimmers – and shrubs and plants for the pixies to hide in, then ambush each other. Which is what pixies like doing.

But the best thing, the very best thing of all – the Frixies have put spycams in the Sanctuary, filming the pixies all day and night. And they stream the film for Frixies to watch at home.

Which I do. An hour a day at least.

So I know every inch of the Sanctuary – and that's why my head was spinning. Because the Sanctuary was where me and Grandma were right now. Grandma put a finger to her lips and got out her wand. She pointed it up at a tiny grey cloud in the sky, waved her wand, muttered magic words, then – a sprinkle of stardust and the cloud came scudding over and parked itself right in front of the spycam.

I knew why.

So trespassers could NOT be seen.

Then Grandma started her trespassing. She tiptoed towards the gate with her wand stretched out. And once again did a spell.

Click. The padlock came off.

I tiptoed after her, half shocked, half thrilled. What was Grandma up to? She wasn't going to *steal* a pixie? Surely not! No. Not even Grandma would do that.

I had no clue how long a witchkid might get in prison for trespassing at a top-secret location. And I had no clue what Grandma was up to – but I didn't care. Not as long as I got to see a forest pixie.

Which I did. In fact, I saw seven.

Seven of them. *Seven.*

Seven forest pixies. Small as my forearm.

Round heads. Huge eyes. Huge ears – well, huge on a pixie. And a big, bright yellowy-green tuft of hair sticking up between the ears.

Small, hairy bodies. Long arms for swinging; long legs for climbing. Strong fingers, strong toes – gripping fingers, gripping toes. And, swishing behind every pixie, a long, long tail.

I could hardly breathe.

I crouched behind a bush and watched as the

pixies jabbered and argued, like pixies do. Shouting and barging, pushing and jostling. All trying to be first up the tree.

Then they were off. All seven. Climbing and climbing, chattering and jabbering, digging in with their long toes, until they were tiny dots. Dots right up on the highest branch of the tree. All lined up in a row.

The pixies all swished their tails. All curled them round the branch. All started to shriek. . .

I was tingling. I really was. Because I knew what was about to happen. And I was here – not watching the Sanctuary on the witchfixer. Actually *here*.

I don't speak Pixish – who does? – but I knew what those shrieks from way up high were all about. The pixies were counting down.

Five … four … three … two … one…

Then they all jumped.

Seven forest pixies threw themselves off the very top branch of the tree. Came hurtling down, shrieking and yelping and whooping – then, just centimetres from the ground. . .

Boing!

The pixies went shooting straight back up again.

Because forest pixies have the stretchiest tails of any creature in the whole of Witchworld. They curl those tails round branches – then jump.

They always judge it perfectly, and they did today.

Up and down they went – *boing, boing, boing, boing* – bouncing back up to the top, then back down to the bottom, again and again.

And when the last *boing* was done, they all climbed up their own tails back to the top branch. They uncurled their tails…

And jumped off again.

I watched, so thrilled I could hardly breathe. I watched as seven pixies, huge ears flapping, came swooping and gliding and shrieking from the top of the tree, right down to the ground.

It was the best moment of my life. EVER.

So I turned to Grandma to give her a hug – but she wasn't there.

Grandma was gone.

Chapter 5

GRATED DRAGON'S TOOTH

DRIED TROLL TOENAILS

Grandma wasn't gone far. I found her darting from bush to bush, creeping towards a log lying on the ground. The Frixies have stuck a little sign next to the log:

PLUCKY'S PLACE

Plucky's Place! I crept fast as I could to join her. Plucky was headline news in South Witchenland. He made the front page of the *Daily Wail*:

PLUCKY PIXIE MAKES IT TO CAMP!

Which is how he got his name.

Because the Frixies saved ninety-four pixies from the Freefall Forest fire and they thought that was all of them. But it wasn't. There was one more.

And he turned up – two whole years after the fire – outside the Sanctuary. A tiny pixie, whimpering and limping and clearly exhausted.

Plucky.

It's a mystery how Plucky made it from Freefall Forest to the Sanctuary. According to the Frixies he must have travelled over seven hundred kilometres – and a lot of that's mountains and forests.

Plucky couldn't have walked it all. Not even in two years. So maybe he stowed away on skyriders. Maybe he grabbed hold of the tail of a passing unicorn, or the claws of a shrikkwarble. Who knows?

But the Frixies have taken good care of poor Plucky. He's got a special little den in the log, because he's limping too much to do any tree climbing.

He stays in his den most of the time. The Frixies have put in lots of stuff to make him comfortable. He sleeps a lot. He eats a lot. And the other pixies pop in and out all day long, bringing him little treats.

The first night Plucky arrived, all the pixies

gathered round him and he started squeaking. And you didn't have speak Pixish to realise he was telling them about his journey.

It must have been quite some journey because all the pixies kept gasping and clutching each other, and three times in his story all the pixies started quaking and their teeth started clattering – so he clearly *was* a plucky pixie.

At the end of it, Plucky must have told them tragic news about his family. Because one by one the pixies started sobbing, and blowing their noses on petals, and putting their arms round him. All nodding, like they understood, like they'd suffered tragic losses too.

And after that Plucky limped off alone, head drooping. To the one little corner of the wood where the spycams don't film – a dark, overgrown corner, all brambles and thorns. Plucky stayed there an hour. Alone.

He must like it there. He goes there every day. Always at dusk. Always alone.

The Frixies think Plucky must have lost his whole family in the Freefall Forest fire. And that's why he goes off – to grieve.

Plucky. The miracle pixie. And I was about to see him.

Me and Grandma tiptoed over, crouched down and peered in.

There he was. Plucky.

Lying flat on his back under a warm red light. Covered in a tiny soft blanket. Snoring gently. Mouth wide open, huge eyes tight shut, ears stretched out sideways across the pillow.

I could see tiny details. The softness, the fluffiness of his little hairy body. His enormous eyelids, his curling eyelashes, jet black and long as my nail. His tiny nostrils, flaring in and out as he breathed.

Grandma got something out of her robe. A bag.

She rustled it.

What was it? A snack, a treat?

I edged closer. Any second now I could watch Plucky – a real live forest pixie – nibbling on Grandma's forest pixie treat. And close up, so close I'd be able to see every nibble of Plucky's tiny sharp teeth, hear every munch.

Then Grandma opened the bag.

What would the treat be? Nuts? Berries?

Oh…

What was it? It didn't smell fresh or woodlandy, or like anything a forest pixie would want to eat. It smelt of rotting. Like something dead. A dead rotting fish, dead rotting flesh.

What was Grandma doing? Trying to *poison* Plucky?

Plucky opened one eye, one huge round eye – bright blue, edged with yellow, and a jet-black middle.

Then Plucky opened the other eye.

He stared at Grandma without blinking. He stared at the bag. His little nostrils gave a twitch. He started licking his lips.

He looked hungry. Eager to eat.

Now, *that* was a surprise. Because I have memorised the complete list of Forest Pixie Fave Foods that the Frixies put on the witchweb. And rotting things are NOT on that list.

"I knew it," whispered Grandma, and her eyes started gleaming. "I knew it!"

But I had no time to ask what she knew because things happened VERY fast after that.

First, Grandma lunged forwards. Second, she clapped a hand over Plucky's mouth. And third, she yanked at his head – hard – and pulled one of the bright yellowy-green tufts of hair right out.

Then she scuttled off fast as she could, heading back to her broomstick.

Chapter 6

"I'm reporting you!" I yelled over Grandma's shoulder as the broomstick took off. "I'm handing you over to a witchwarden! Poor, *poor* Plucky!"

"Poor Plucky?" Grandma yelled back as we lurched up into the sky. "Nothing poor – nothing plucky – WHATSOEVER about that ghastly little creature!"

I clung on. Plucky? A ghastly little creature? How could Grandma say that? Plucky wasn't ghastly. Plucky was lovely.

"Pixie tormentor!" I yelled in her ear.

"Pixie?" Grandma yelled back as the broomstick

gave a sideways lurch. "Pixie! *Pah!* If that – that *thing* was a pixie then I am a boiled striggle egg!"

"Grandma!" I yelled, clutching on to her even harder and trying not to look at Witchworld rushing past. "What are you talking about? Why did you pull Plucky's hair out? Why?"

"Because that hair – that one hair, could save us all!" Grandma yelled as the broomstick lurched back the way we came.

Save us?

"Save us?" I yelled. "Save us from *what*?" But I had a horrible feeling I knew the answer.

And I did.

"Ghouls, of course," yelled Grandma. "GHOULS!"

Ghouls. Plucky's hair could save us from ghouls.

As if.

I yelled at Grandma all the way home. I yelled a LOT.

I yelled that I was reporting her to the Frixies for cruelty to pixies.

I yelled that I was reporting her to Witchkidline for cruelty to granddaughters. And also to witchwardens for forcing a witchkid to become an underage robber and criminal.

I even yelled – and I'm not proud of this – that

Grandma should NOT be living in my house because she should be living in Heckles Haghome, along with all the other troublesome old witchladies who talked nonsense all day.

And Grandma yelled back that she had to get home fast, and had no time to waste explaining herself to a cross little witchgirl shouting rude things in her ear.

Then she leaned right over her broomstick and ignored me all the way home. She also got her revenge for my yelling. Because she sent the broomstick lurching off Skyway 121 and down to the garden – but did she come in for a landing? No. She did a loop-the-loop.

No warning. No telling me to hold on tight. Nothing.

She just sent her broomstick spinning in a big swooping loop. So – of course – I lost my grip and fell off. *Again*.

Only this time I fell off straight into our garden pond.

And Grandma hovered over me, looking extremely pleased with herself. "See," she said smugly. "I said you wouldn't fall off on landing the second time. And you didn't. Because you fell off *before* landing."

Then she went indoors, cackling, as if she'd made

a very good joke. Which she hadn't.

✦

Forty-three minutes. That's how long I had to spend in the shower to get rid of the smell of our pond.

But, finally, I came out of the bathroom smelling of soap and cleanness, instead of slime and mud and fish stink.

Then I stomped off to Mum's office – because Mum works from home some of the time – switched on her witchfixer, and half an hour later I went to see Grandma.

"Grandma," I said. "I've been checking. There are over two hundred million entries on the witchweb about ghouls. And every single one says the same thing. Ghouls are EXTINCT."

Grandma just snorted.

"They all died in the Great Ghoul War," I said. "In a very big magiquake."

Now, not one of you witchkids needs telling about magiquakes. Whether you're reading this in Grittenglidd, or Frakkenwild, or wherever, you'll know about magiquakes.

Witchkids *all* know. Know what it's like living on a globe sizzling with magic, in its rocks, in its trees, in its gases. In everything. Know about the sudden surges of magical power – and the astonishing sights, the mindboggling events those surges can cause.

Including magiquakes.

Like the one that finished off the ghouls. A vast crack, jagged and wide and deep, that surged across that battlefield in the Great Ghoul War. Split the battlefield in two. Then scooped them all up – ghouls, witches, all of them – swallowed them down and snapped itself shut. Buried them deep underground.

"And, Grandma," I said. "I've printed out *proof* they are extinct for you."

I put the proof in Grandma's hand. The species certificate for ghouls. With a big picture of a ghoul. And, underneath – the current E status of ghouls.

Not Existing, like frogs and yafflepecks and unicorns.

Not Endangered, like forest pixies.

NO.

There, in big black letters, on the certificate. The current E status of ghouls.

EXTINCT

But Grandma just looked at it – and snorted more.

"Grandma, stop snorting," I said, fed up now, because she shouldn't be snorting at such an important certificate. "This is issued by the Unity of Colonies – the *most important organisation* in the whole of Witchworld. And signed by the Witchglobe Guardian."

"And THAT is your proof?" Grandma said.

Then she slapped a huge sheet of paper in my hand. "Flo, your proof is *faulty*," she said. "Keep alert at all times. And if you spot any of these, tell me."

I looked down, even more fed up. All that effort with my proof, and Grandma just ignored it.

As for this… Grandma had drawn out two shapes. Two huge shapes. Wide webbed foot with six long toes.

Ghoul footprints.

"Grandma," I said crossly. "These are *enormous*. Something that made these footprints would have to be the size of a small giant."

"An average ghoul, Flo, is two metres tall," said Grandma. "With huge hands the size of shovels. And right now, somewhere underground, ghouls are using those huge hands to DIG THEIR WAY OUT."

I scowled at Grandma. Because – without me having any choice whatsoever – my knees were knocking.

"Let me tell you a bit more about ghouls, Flo,"

Grandma snapped, right in my face. "Ghouls – huge, towering ghouls – can send witches spinning with one swipe of their knobbly ghoul fists. And ghouls BITE witches. Turn witches into ghouls themselves. And these ghouls will be *desperate* to bite. These ghouls have been underground for almost a thousand years. These ghouls—"

"Grandma, STOP," I said, pointing at my knocking knees. "Look. Look! Stop scaring me. It's not *fair*."

"You *should* be scared, Flo," Grandma said. "You should be VERY scared. Ghouls are nearly here. And when they are – who will be their first witchvictims? Witches, here in Haggspit! And their favourite witchvictims? Witchchildren!"

I backed away. I could feel my hair actually standing on end now. But Grandma hadn't finished.

"Read this!" she barked, handing me a copy of her ghoul booklet. "Read this and learn! Read this before those ghouls come prowling and sniffing and searching for witchchildren – small, juicy witchchildren to grab! Wriggling, squirming, screaming witchchildren. Witchchildren like YOU!"

I'd heard enough. I turned and ran. Hurled myself out of Grandma's room, through the house and into my bedroom. Then I slammed the door shut.

Chapter 7

GRATED DRAGON'S TOOTH

DRIED TROLL TOE NAILS

My room is big and my bed is high. A bunk bed, with a whoosher up to it – but the whoosher's not working too well at the moment. Sometimes it whooshes out of the window and round the garden, instead of up to bed.

There's a space under my bed. A little room all its own. With two short sides – a desk built into one, my big board of pictures on the other – and a long squishy seat between them.

Which I curled myself up on.

I did NOT want to think about Grandma, about her ghoul talk, her ghoul booklet, not for one more minute. So I stared at my big board of pictures – lots and lots of pictures, ones that mean stuff to me.

Mainly pictures of Dad.

Dad on his own, doing Dad-things – painting, planting diggle seeds, playing the firkelhorn.

Dad with Mum. Both laughing, both young. And Hetty there too, a tiny witchbaby in a big black pram.

Dad with Grandma, having a wand lesson, with a pointy black hat on his head. Because Dad was a big fan of Grandma. Dad and Grandma would chat for hours.

"Never laugh at the ways of old witches," Dad was always telling me and Hetty. "Your grandmother knows more about spells, more about potions, more about Witchworld than most."

But then Dad had never heard Grandma going on about ghouls.

I sniffed. I never know if it's good to look at my pictures, or bad. If it makes me feel better, or worse.

There are lots of pictures of me with Dad. Lots and lots.

Me, a witchtoddler-me, sitting on Dad's lap, him reading me a picture book about windwhirls.

Me with Dad at our villa in Kronebay, slithering through the garden, pretending to be sea serpents.

Witchworld

Me with Dad at Oggentakk Zoo, three Lakktarnian skrangotts swinging through the trees behind us.

Me with Dad picnicking by the Singing Stillwaters.

And my favourite. My absolute favourite.

Me with Dad and Hetty. All jumping off a rock, all arms in the air, all in mid-leap – all shouting and screaming with laughter.

A day I have never, EVER forgotten. The day me, Dad and Hetty flew to Krokkenridge Rock.

Krokkenridge Rock is in Witchenfinn. A tall, tall rock, on the edge of a lagoon.

Witchkids jump off Krokkenridge Rock all the time. Daring witchkids, like Hetty. And Hetty couldn't wait to get there. She went straight up to the top, and jumped.

I took one look over the edge, and stepped back. "No, Dad," I said. "I can't jump off there. I *can't*."

Hours I sat, on the edge of Krokkenridge Rock, staring down.

Sometimes I almost jumped. Sometimes I didn't. And for hours, Hetty jumped. Other witchkids jumped. Witchdads, witchmums, witchteens, they all jumped.

But not me.

Then Dad came and crouched down next to me.

"Dad," I told him. "I'm so scared. I'll never jump. It's too high."

"Flo," said Dad, smiling at me. "Here's what you do. Imagine a future."

"Imagine a *future?*" I said.

Dad nodded. "Imagine a future where you DO that jump," he said. "Imagine how you'll feel."

So I did. I imagined going home that night, telling Mum about how I did the jump. Imagined going to sleep knowing I did the jump, how proud I would feel.

"Now ask yourself one simple question, Flo," said Dad. "What future do you want? That future? The one where you do the jump? Or another future? One where you don't do the jump?"

Well, that was easy.

"*That* future," I said. "The future where I *do* the jump."

"Then create that future," Dad said, smiling more. "Because you *can*, Flo. Some futures you can MAKE happen – like this one."

Well, that was easy for Dad to say.

"But Dad," I said, shaking my head. "It's too high. I'm not brave. I can't do it."

"Not brave, Flo?" Dad said, looking astonished, but I didn't know why. "You are brave every day."

44

I shook my head. "I'm NOT, Dad," I said. "I'm scared of almost *everything*. Talking in front of the whole class. Walking round corners. Waking up at night, knowing everyone else is asleep. Half the things I *do* make me scared."

Then I watched as Hetty hurled herself off the edge again. "See," I said. "Hetty's the brave one."

Now Dad was shaking his head. "There's nothing brave about jumping if it doesn't scare you," he said. "It's fun. It's exciting. But it's not brave.

"Flo," Dad said, putting his arm round me and smiling again. "It's witchgirls who do things when they're scared – they're the TRULY brave ones."

And I did it. I stood on that edge. Looked down at that long, long drop. Thought again and again about what Dad had said.

Then I jumped.

I jumped all day after that. Alone. With Hetty. With Dad. And then we all jumped together, and another witchdad took the picture.

Hetty has that picture too.

But last year – one year exactly after Dad was gone – she took it down. And when I asked her why, she glared at me.

"Because Dad is gone – and there is not ONE thing I can do about it," she said. "So I do *not* want to see that picture any more. I do *not* want to think about Dad. And I do *not* want to talk about Dad."

And Hetty never does.

So I sat there, and looked at my pictures, and I sniffed.

Then I sniffed again.

I could smell something. A horrible something. A smell wafting out of the kitchen and right through the house.

A smell of burning and mould and rotting things. A smell of old gripball robes left in a bag too long. Of poop pats left by a boggle with tummy trouble. Of goblins' earwax fried up in a pan.

And I knew straight away. That smell was something to do with Grandma.

Chapter 8

GRATED DRAGON'S TOOTH

DRIED TROLL TOENAILS

I stood in the kitchen doorway and gaped. Mum's kitchen is stuffed with the latest gadgets, with an enormous witchscreen on one wall. And usually Mum's kitchen is shiny and gleaming and clean.

Not now it wasn't.

Because Grandma had got busy, sorting herself out a corner. And Grandma's corner was groaning with battered old pots and pans. There were shelves stuffed with spell books and potion books. And three giant spiders dozing in cages.

Measuring cups and weights and spoons were spilling all over Mum's worktop. And jars were

open, lots of them. Jars with labels in Grandma's
spidery writing.

```
pickled serpent fangs
dried troll toenails
grated dragon teeth
sliced fairy droppings
mermaid scales, assorted sizes
```

And right in the middle of Mum's new flagstone
floor, Grandma had plonked a grate. A heavy metal
grate with a fire flaming in it — and Grandma's
biggest cauldron bubbling and steaming above it.

With Grandma standing there, stirring and
mixing, putting in a pinch of this, a pinch of that,
checking and rechecking her potion book.

And frogs. There were frogs.

Everywhere.

Frogs in the cauldron, frogs doing front crawl and
backstroke and breaststroke, frogs treading water,
frogs jumping in. Frogs climbing a little ladder to a
high diving board. Frogs on the floor. Frogs curled
up asleep in a frog basket.

I have never seen so many frogs in one place.

Just then I heard the sound of a skyshredder
parking. Then footsteps, clacking high heels, heading

for the back door. And in walked Mum, then Hetty – both carrying huge heavy shopping bags.

They gaped, just like I did. Every single shopping bag hit the floor with a clunk.

"No, Grandma!" Hetty wailed. "It's too smelly! Too steamy! My hair! It'll droop! My hair!" Then she bolted for the kitchen door.

As for Mum, she started fanning herself with a tea towel, as if she was overheating. And I could see her grinding her teeth.

She stomped over to the cupboard by the witchowave. "One word, Mother," she screeched, flinging open the cupboard door and pointing. "Potions2Go!"

Because Mum has a cupboard full of Potions2Go. She's always ordering them off the witchweb. Best of all the ready-potions, she says – expensive, but worth it.

Grandma ignored her.

She got a big spoon with holes in it, scooped all the frogs out of the spitting, hissing cauldron and carefully put them on the floor. "Off you go then," she said, smiling fondly. "Outside."

The frogs all hopped off to the back door. Then they started throwing themselves at it, and bouncing off it, croaking and glaring at Grandma.

"Kristabel," said Grandma, frowning at Mum. "Where's your frog flap?"

Now Mum started wailing. "Mother," she wailed. "Witches don't *need* frog flaps. Not any more."

"Well, I'm a witch and I need a frog flap," said Grandma, eyes popping.

Mum was bright green now, and snarling. She waved a ready-potion in Grandma's face, ripped the box open and pulled out the potion pouch. "See?" she said. "*See!* One ready-potion!"

Then she pulled out the little sachet that always comes with ready-potions. "And this," she hissed, waving it at Grandma. "This – do you know what this is? Powdered frog essence!

"Mix them together," Mum said – no, screeched. "Ten seconds in the witchowave – done! No fuss. No mess. And NO FROGS!"

Grandma just snorted. "Do you know *nothing* about frog farms, Kristabel?" she said. "Those poor little frogs. Short, miserable lives – two thousand to a cage. No fresh air. No daylight. Then BAKED. Baked, and ground up into powder. It's a *disgrace*."

Then Grandma pulled herself up to her full height – which isn't much, as she's no taller than I am. She glared at Mum. "My frogs roam free," she said proudly, then waved her wand.

"Nooooo," wailed Mum.

"Abrakkida Flarannik, Appetikki Portik," said Grandma. "Antik Non, Antek Non, Timune." And, with a whoosh of stardust, the back door – Mum's designer cave-style door, the door Mum spent a fortune shipping in from Shivergrim – had a small green frog flap in it.

Mum made a *grrrrrr* sort of noise, slapped her hand against her head and swirled off out of the kitchen.

Chapter 9

Close up, the potion was black as darkness. Bubbling and steaming and stinking. And Grandma's potion book was lying open on the worktop.

Mum has potion books, but they just sit in a cupboard and hardly ever get used. Grandma's potion book looked as if it was used every day. As if it had been used every day for the last hundred years.

It was a huge tatty thing. The page edges were all curled up and yellowed. It had splodges of potion all over it – and it was open at a page with swirly old-fashioned writing on it.

DOPPEL POTION
A potion that disguiseth
a witch

Then a list. An extremely long list. Thirty ingredients at least. Including, right at the very end, one that caught my eye.

a hair from a doppel's head

A hair. From a doppel's head...

I looked in the silver jar next to the potion book. At the tuft of yellowy-green hair, lying on a tiny cushion...

I thought back. At how Grandma looked as she saw Plucky sniffing at whatever was in her bag. At her whispered words. "*I knew it, I knew it.*"

Oh dear.

I was beginning to understand – although I wished I wasn't.

"Grandma," I said carefully. "Plucky's hair... Why exactly did you steal it?"

"For this potion, of course," said Grandma. Then she jabbed her finger at the list of ingredients.

"There," she said. "There. Plain as your face. The final ingredient – a hair from a doppel's head."

"So, Grandma…" I said. "You think – you actually think – that Plucky, poor little Plucky, Plucky the pixie, is really a *doppel?*"

Grandma's eyes gleamed at me. "I don't think," she said. "I *know*."

Yes.

Grandma had done it again.

Because every witchkid older than three knows five basic facts about doppels.

One – they're fat grey maggots born from rotting things.

Two – they're shapeshifting maggots.

Three – they shapeshift to join a herd – any herd, goblins, fairies, dragons, trolls, they're not fussy – and pretend to be sick, so they get looked after.

Four – they have to change back into a maggot for one hour each day or they explode.

And five – well, you don't need me to tell you five.

Doppels are EXTINCT.

"Grandma," I said. "Doppels died out in the Second Ice Age."

Grandma's eyebrows shot up over her specs. "And what is left over from the Second Ice Age?" she said. "The Frozen Wastes!"

Well, yes. We saw a documentary about it in witchcitizenship class. How in the Second Ice Age the whole of Witchworld was Frozen Wastes. And the Frozen Wastes we have now are the leftovers.

But Grandma hadn't finished. "And what are the Frozen Wastes doing?" she said. "Melting!"

Yes again. They *are* melting, bits of them, because of how witches all live. That's what the documentary was about. About snow witches. Those strange pale witches. The ones who live above the Iceline and dress in white fur robes. About the threat to their way of life.

"Well then," said Grandma triumphantly. "That's where the doppel was. Frozen in the ice. The ice melts. The doppel thaws. Simple."

"But, Grandma," I said. "Even if a doppel DID thaw, the Frozen Wastes are over two thousand five hundred miles from South Witchenland – which is a long way for a maggot to crawl and swim. So how would it get to the Sanctuary?"

"Doppels have ways," Grandma said darkly – as if that was an answer.

"The second I heard about that pixie, I knew," Grandma said, eyes gleaming. "The mystery arrival. The limping. The pretending to be sick. Classic signs – every one of them."

"But, Grandma," I said, baffled. "*Why* exactly are you making a doppel potion?"

"It is part of the fight against ghouls!" said Grandma.

"But—" I said.

"Not now, Flo," said Grandma, holding up a hand. "I have work to do. My doppel potion is almost ready."

Then she sniffed and she stirred and she nodded. "The most perfect, astonishing potion," she said proudly. "One only the greatest of witches can make."

Which was when the potion started making noises. Strange, whining, whimpering noises – almost as if there was a herd of creatures, very unhappy creatures, trapped in there.

"Oh," said Grandma, looking surprised. She checked her potions book, then rechecked. She frowned.

"Is this the first time you've made doppel potion, Grandma?" I said. "Because it doesn't sound very happy."

"There is a first time for everything," said Grandma serenely. Then she opened the small silver jar – and out came the hair. Poor Plucky's tiny tuft of hair.

"Stand back, Flo," Grandma said.

And she dropped Plucky's hair into the cauldron. Into that bubbling, steaming, stinking potion.

The potion exploded.

Big bubbles shot out of it. Black shiny bubbles, big as gripballs. Bubbles that exploded all over the kitchen. Exploded like fireworks, bursting into colours and shapes. Swirling shapes. Shapes moving so fast, changing so quickly I could hardly make out what they were.

Shapes of snarling teeth and glowing eyes and stamping hooves. Shapes of dragons and trolls and mermaids. Shapes of goblins and werewolves and ogres. Shapes of unicorns and griffins and serpents. Shapes of windsniffers and gritterbacks and thrumbulgers…

It was a spectacular sight, an astonishing sight. Shape after shape after shape. So maybe that was why – just for a second – a thought sneaked into my head.

Could Grandma be right? About doppels? About ghouls?

But then the thought was gone. Because Grandma was NOT right. I knew she wasn't.

And a ghoul attack, right here in Haggspit – well,

that was about as likely as me, Florence Skritchett, becoming the saviour of Witchworld.

Part
Two

Chapter
10

Lily Jaggwort and Kika Rorrit-Mogg have been my friends since we were witchbabies. We met at Upper Haggspit Medicentre, having our first injections against grindle fever, skids and whooping shrieks. Our mums got talking, and they've been friends ever since.

So have me and Lily and Kika.

Tonight was Lily's birthday sleepover – and I was glad to get out of my house, away from Grandma and her stinking potion. Glad to be going...

Until I got there.

Usually at sleepovers me and Lily and Kika do fun

stuff. Like making giant carrot costumes and wearing them to the shops. Or speaking grinthoggish for an hour – oinking and grunting only.

But tonight we did NOT do fun stuff. Not at all. And it was all the fault of the Book. The stupid, stupid Book.

Kika's present to Lily.

"Lils," said Kika, and her eyes were actually shining as she handed over her present, oblong and bulky, and wrapped in green paper with hearts all over it. "You will totally love this."

Lily took the present. She shook it, she squeezed it – and I saw her eyes narrow. Then she frowned. "Kika," she said sternly. "This feels like a book. You *know* I don't read books. Not ever."

"Oh, you so *will* read this book," said Kika, clasping her hands together. "Trust me. You SO will."

And Kika was right. Lily *did* read the book. For hours…

Two Hundred Utterly Important Things a Witchgirl Should Know – that was the title.

But the title was wrong. Because there was not one utterly important thing in it. Nothing useful, like how to splint a broken dragon's wing. Or ten ways to tame a gurtle. Or top tips for developing X-ray vision. Not one.

No. Just utterly *not*-important things – like how to have the scraggiest hairdo. What to do when you like a witchboy. Five fun ways to jazz up last year's robes.

Dull, dull, DULL.

But Lily and Kika didn't think so. Which meant, in the next three hours, we did the quiz on page 35 – What's *your* type? – to find our perfect witchboy. Then we had to practise walking with confidence – page 22. And we also did a soothing foot massage – page 53 – which I found ticklish and not at all soothing.

And then Lily made a bowl of gloop – as shown on page 17 – with the following ingredients:

one pomegranate, squished
three pickled dewdrops
four dried bat wings, crushed
one pelloligan egg, whisked
two tablespoons of whirtle syrup
three generous handfuls of nettles

Then she started smearing the gloop all over my face.

I groaned. I couldn't help it. "I don't want that stuff on my face," I said. "And I'm fed up with the Book."

Kika gasped. "Flo," she said – shocked, for some reason. "Don't you want gorgeous, glowing green skin?"

"No," I said. "Can't we do something that *isn't* the Book? We've been doing stuff from the Book all evening. I want to play Pixie Panix IV."

Pixie Panix IV was my present to Lily. The brand-new edition of the forest pixie game – action-packed, with new choices of pixie to be, new locations, new baddies, exploding toadstools, and goblins to zap.

"Flo," said Lily. "It's *my* birthday sleepover and *I* want us to do the fifteen-minute face mask. So sit still."

Then she smeared the gloopy stuff all over my face, then over Kika's face, then her own. And we had to sit for fifteen whole minutes while the gloopy stuff dried. And we couldn't even talk because talking would crack the fifteen-minute face mask.

Worse, we didn't play Pixie Panix IV, because Lily's auntie had given her another game, Date Fate. So we played that instead. And Date Fate was just lots of choosing. Choosing outfits. Choosing witchboys. Choosing where to go on the date. Choosing whether to stand your date up. Choosing whether to double date…

It was even duller than the Book.

AND – playing Date Fate made us miss *Skyhunter*, which is my favourite show on the witchscreen.

Skyhunter, if you don't get it in your colony, is about a fearless witchkid, Destiny Daggett. She works for the government and roams around Witchworld sorting out villains. Each week Destiny ends up in deadly peril, and each week she sorts out the deadly peril by being brave and daring.

I could never be brave and daring like Destiny, but I do like watching *her* be it.

But not tonight.

No Destiny, no *Skyhunter*. Just hours and hours of Date Fate. And I got so bored I fell asleep – but then I dreamed the ghoul on the front of Grandma's booklet came to life, and stepped off the page...

So I woke up, shrieking about ghouls.

And Lily stopped playing Date Fate, looked at me and frowned. "Ghouls?" she said. "No, Flo, no no. Ghouls are a nightmare for teeny-tiny witchkids. Not for witchgirls our age."

The next morning, me and Lily and Kika went to Snappy Snax in the mall for shivershakes. And straight off, Lily and Kika started talking about Wednesday. So I groaned. Again.

"Can we NOT talk about Wednesday?" I said.

Lily's eyebrows shot up. "Why not?" she said.

"I don't want to," I said. "I don't even want to think about it."

Because Wednesday is the day we look round upper schools for next year. Lily and Kika can't wait to be upper learners and go to upper school, but I can. I like being a lower learner, and being in our lower school – Charms.

"Well then," said Lily. "If we're not talking about Wednesday, I have another idea."

And out came the Book from Lily's bag.

I couldn't help it. Not a groan this time – but a yelp came out of my mouth. A yelp of pain.

Lily glared at me. "Shush, Flo," she said. "This Book is the way forward. We *need* the Book. We are witchgirls at a crucial age. We are *changing*. Growing up. It's just you're a bit slow at it."

Kika clasped my hand. "Growing up can be hard, Flo," she said – and she had this look on her face, which I think was Kika trying to appear wise and understanding. "Sometimes you may feel lonely and confused. You may feel scared of the challenges ahead. This is quite natural. These feelings will pass."

I gaped at Kika. "Are you quoting the Book at me?" I said.

Kika nodded. "Page ninety-one," she said proudly. "Facing new challenges."

"And now," said, Lily, opening the Book up at page 64 – Putting the fizz and fun in fashion – "I have birthday money to spend."

Then she pursed her mouth up and frowned down at the Book. "Choices, choices," she said. "Which shall I get? Glamtastically gruesome earrings or brilliantly biting bangles?"

And when I left to go home – which was soon – Lily and Kika were already planning Monday's thrilling activities. "During lunch break," said Lily, "we are going to practise exiting elegantly from a skyswaggerer."

"And also," added Kika, "our celebrity signatures."

Which was all on page 48 – Handling sudden stardom.

But Monday didn't turn out quite like that...

Chapter 11

On Monday morning I was sitting at the kitchen table, eating breakfast and watching the yafflepeck, up in the woldenbore tree.

The yafflepeck moved into our garden this year. It's a red bird with a plump body and bright-green wings. And it's small, the smallest bird in South Witchenland – but that doesn't seem to bother the yafflepeck. It's the first to start singing every morning; it sings noisily all day and it struts around our garden, bossing all the bigger birds about.

It's clearly very, VERY proud of being a yafflepeck.

Mum came rushing in, scooping up things up for work and flicking backwards and forwards through a pile of papers that said SCHEDULE: MONDAY on the top one.

"I shall be late, I shall be *late*, Flo," she was saying. Which is what Mum says most mornings – and she nearly always *is* late.

Then I heard slow, shuffling feet and Grandma came staggering in. Carrying a very tall stack of paper. So tall she had to peer out from round the side to see where she was going.

She dumped the stack on the worktop.

"Kristabel," said Grandma, marching over and whipping SCHEDULE: MONDAY out of Mum's hands. "There are more important things to do than work today."

Then she pointed at the stack of paper. "One of these must go out to every single household on Moaning Mountain. Witchchildren MUST be safe."

Yes.

Grandma had *another* booklet – and on the front it said this:

WITCHCHILDREN!
EVACUATION –
OR EXTERMINATION!

Now Grandma wanted every witchkid in Haggspit to be evacuated. To leave their witchmums and witchdads, leave their homes, leave their schools and go and stay somewhere else — somewhere NOT in danger of a ghoul attack.

Grandma's booklet had lots of useful evacuation packing tips. Also advice about ghoul goggles, ghoul masks and neck protectors. A tear-off section for witchkids to give to their grown-ups. A list of evacuation dates by area of Haggspit — so evacuation could be orderly. A map of fastest routes out of Haggspit, and a big circle of how far away witchkids should evacuate to…

Oh, and a note that any witchkid with relatives above the Iceline should go there — that being the safest place, as ghouls like heat.

"Evacuation must start this week," said Grandma.

"This week?" said Mum in a dangerously quiet voice.

"Yes, Kristabel," said Grandma. "It is the middle of summer, but there are trees in the Forest of Fears — a very large clump of them — whose leaves have turned. Become autumn leaves. And why? Because the ground is extremely CHILLY. Because ghouls are near the surface. And when they reach it — a ghoul attack!"

70

"A ghoul attack?" said Mum with dangerously glinting eyes.

"Indeed," nodded Grandma. "No witchchild is safe. The ghoul attack could be anywhere in Haggspit. Flo's school. Hetty's school. Haggspit Baths. Anywhere witchchildren gather. And we must be prepared. I shall need witches. Thousands of them."

"You will?" said Mum, a dangerously sarcastic note creeping into her voice now.

Grandma doesn't do sarcasm. "Yes, Kristabel," she said. "You can't get rid of ghouls with a tiny bit of magic. Ghouls are strong. Strong in body. Strong against magic. I shall need thousands and *thousands* of witches. All doing the same spell."

Then she prodded Mum. "You can do that. Get your silly readers to do something useful for once."

"I can?" said Mum, teeth clenching. "And what spell will that be exactly?"

"How do I know?" said Grandma, eyes popping. "Really, Kristabel, must I do everything? Think, think!"

"I *AM* thinking," Mum hissed, looking truly dangerous now. "I am thinking that this – *this*, Mother – is the most important week of my entire year. This is the week I prepare for Conference!"

Conference.

Mum goes to Conference every year. Conference takes a whole weekend and I think Conference is where all the magazine bosses boast to each other about how good their magazine is and how many readers they have. And there's a big dinner at Conference and prizes.

The week before Conference, Mum is always tired and grumpy. So this was *not* a good week for Grandma to go on about ghouls.

"Conference is my big chance to shine!" hissed Mum. "My chance to impress. I will NOT have you interfering with Conference!"

"Conference is not as important as ghouls," said Grandma firmly. Then she turned to me. "And you, Flo," she said. "No school today. Not for you, not for Hetty. Skritchetts must deliver these. There is no time to waste."

Mum's mouth dropped open.

"No school?" she said. "No work? No school?" And her teeth were beginning to gnash.

"No," said Grandma. Then she pointed at Mum's skychatter. "Use the thingy. Tell that office of yours you have booklets to deliver."

"Booklets! *Ghoul* booklets?" hissed Mum. "To

DELIVER?"

Mum was seriously in danger of exploding. She had gone a deep, dark green. Smoke was shooting out of both ears, then she whipped out her spellstick. Her fingers went flying. And whatever spell Mum was planning to do, it was big, a three-parter at least.

Then Mum pointed her spellstick. "Abrakkida Rune," she hissed – and the whole pile of booklets started ripping themselves into shreds, the shreds turned themselves into flapping paper birds, and they all flew off out of the window.

"THAT," Mum screeched, "is what I think of your booklets!"

Mum was too angry to say another word. She just stood there, slapping her hand against her head and – once again – making that strangled *grrrrr* noise.

But just then her skychatter pinged.

There was an urgent text from my school.

A nest of young gulchers had been discovered in the school kitchens. School was closed until the Department of Witch Wellbeing and Safety was satisfied every single one was gone – and that none of them had slithered into other parts of the building.

Which was how I ended up going to work with Mum.

Chapter 12

"I am NOT leaving you here with that witch, Flo," Mum said, glaring at Grandma and ripping down a poster of ghoul footprints that Grandma had just stuck — face out — in the front porch for witches walking by to see.

"Kristabel," Grandma said, sticking a wand in her pocket and pulling on an extra robe. "I'll come too. We must do something useful with that silly magazine of yours. Put the news out. Warn witches of the ghoul attack."

"You will NOT come too," hissed Mum. "I have a very important meeting this morning. And I will not have you ruining it!"

Then she grabbed my arm. "Flo," she said. "Let's go!" And she marched off to the skyshredder.

But Grandma was marching right behind us — because Grandma had turned herself invisible.

She stowed away.

✦

Mum's office is on the top — tenth — floor of the *Hocus Pocus* tower. It's one huge room with windows all round and desks full of witches at work.

I've been there before and it's always busy. It was now.

Witchfixers were flickering, skychatters were ringing. And a big bank of witchscreens was showing celebrity news channels — Zoe Shreek giving an interview, doing lots of pouting. Kakkle Kru running for a skyswaggerer, being chased by screaming witchteens. . .

And everywhere witches were bustling about, holding bits of paper, shouting into skychatters and looking important.

Mum stood in the middle of the room and clapped her hands. "Team!" she said. "Prepare. Prepare! In ten minutes Mr Potions2Go himself — Meristo Hurlstruk — will be here. We must impress him! We must dazzle!"

Meristo Hurlstruk. The big boss of Potions2Go, over here from Fangway. He was on the witchscreen news last night, droning on about some big plan he had to expand the Potions2Go empire even more in United Witchenlands.

"Remember, girls," said Mum. "Greet him in Fangwegian – *hikkel vartt, hikkel vartt*. Let me hear you."

"*Hikkel vartt*," the witches all started mumbling. "*Hikkel vartt*."

Then Mum cupped a hand to her ear. "I can't hear you," she sang out.

"*HIKKEL VARTT!*" they all shouted. "*HIKKEL VARTT!*"

Mum beamed round the room. "This is our big chance, girls. We must persuade him to spend millions advertising his products in our glorious magazine. And NOT in *Scoop!*"

All the witches started booing when Mum said *Scoop!* Because *Scoop!* is the biggest rival *Hocus Pocus* has. And just as pointless, in my opinion.

One witch put her hand up. "Kristabel," she said nervously. "I think you need to see this." Then she held out a copy of *Scoop!*

"The latest edition," she said. "They've come up with something quite clever."

So Mum looked. Her teeth started gnashing. She flushed dark green. I read over her shoulder. The cover. In big letters.

FREE TO ALL READERS!
POP-UP PAMPER PARTY!
MAKEOVERS!
MASSAGES!
SPA TREATMENTS!
GOODIE BAGS!
EXPERT ADVICE!
BRING THIS ISSUE WITH YOU –
AND IT'S ALL YOURS!

"We should have thought of that," Mum hissed, smoke blasting out of both ears. "This week's circulation figures! They'll double! Just before Conference!"

Mum is always going on about circulation figures, which is – I think – how many copies the magazine sells each week.

"Miranda, Levity, Prue," said Mum, pointing at three witches. "My office now! We need *readers*. New readers! We MUST think of ways to get new readers. We must have exciting plans to announce at Conference."

Then Mum swept across the room to her office, a room on its own, right at the end, behind a glass wall. "Googie," she said, pointing at a young witch sitting at a desk near the door. "Superskinny actojuice, double shot, triple froth, two sweeteners. Now, please. Thank you, darling."

Mum and the three witches sat at her big round table.

"Flo," Mum said, pointing to a couch in the corner. "Meristo Hurlstruk is a family man so sit there, look intelligent, be polite – and impress him with my witchchild-rearing skills."

Then she turned to the three witches at the table. "Girls," she said. "First. Next week's cover story. Something snappy. Something current. Something to draw new readers in. Something brilliant. Ideas?"

Which was when a shimmering black shape began to appear at one of the empty seats. A shimmering black shape in old robes. . .

"Ghouls, Kristabel," said Grandma firmly. "THAT'S your cover story."

Mum shrieked – as loud as ten banshees. Her teeth gnashed. Her face turned a dark poison green, and green flames flickered in both her eyes.

Grandma was in trouble.

"Mother," Mum screeched, advancing on

Grandma. "You have gone TOO FAR!" Then she opened her mouth wide and started hissing.

Grandma wagged her finger. "Kristabel," she said sternly. "Don't you dare."

"Oh, I dare!" screeched Mum, hissing more. "I *dare!*"

Oh no. Oh no no no. I put my head in my hands. Mum couldn't do what I thought she was about to do. She just *couldn't.* Not to Grandma. Surely not. Not to her own mother?

Mum did.

Hissing louder and louder, she raised her arms. She flexed her fingers. She pointed – and lines of thread shot out from every single one of her fingers. Strong sticky thread, the sort spiders spin, heading straight for Grandma...

Araknawitchery is the only sport Mum thinks is worth doing. "Not one of those nasty sports that makes your face all shiny and your robes all muddy," she says. "Just skill and creativity."

Mum won her first araknawitchery medal when she was twelve. By fifteen she was the under-sixteen champion of South Witchenland. An all-rounder, excellent in every category – web spinning, cocooning, targets and artistry. And as skilled with her left hand as she was with the right.

Mum could have had a professional sporting career – but when she was seventeen she gave it all up. "Too much training," she always says. "Not enough fun. And no parties."

But she still has the skills…

It took less than ten seconds before Grandma was wrapped up, trapped, cocooned in spider thread – just her face sticking out, glaring at Mum.

"Why oh why oh *why* do I have you as a mother?" Mum shrieked, right in Grandma's face. "I could have had a lovely mother! But I got you! YOU!"

"This is cruelty!" Grandma yelled at her, struggling. "Cruelty and foolishness!"

"Kristabel," said one of the witches at the table nervously. "I think araknawitchery in the office is a bit … well, illegal."

But Mum didn't care. Mum had lost it. Totally. "Now!" she screeched, then she picked up Grandma, started cackling – quite hysterically – and tucked Grandma under one arm. "Now! To the rubbish chute! Yes! I shall send you down the rubbish chute! And Meristo Hurlstruk will never even know you were here!"

But Mum was wrong.

Because Meristo Hurlstruk was early. Already here. And standing in the doorway with a big frown on his face.

He took one look at Mum, screeching and cackling. One look at Grandma, tucked under Mum's arm, cocooned and struggling.

Then he turned on his heel and walked out.

Things were very *very* frosty on the way home. Mum could barely speak, her teeth were grinding so much.

"I would stick you in Heckles Haghome right now," Mum hissed at Grandma as we swooped along Skyway 172. "Except I can see the *Scoop!* headline already – NO MERCY FOR MAG MOGUL MUM!"

"Mother cocooner!" Grandma snorted. "Ghoul denier! Witchworld destroyer!" Then her mouth snapped shut and she glared out of the flexipod all the way home.

Chapter 13

On Tuesday I woke up because I could smell burning and hear shrieks.

"My wands!" Grandma was shrieking. "My wands! Save them!"

I sprinted along the corridor, and so did Mum. We charged into Grandma's room – Mum first, me following.

Grandma was sitting bolt upright in her bed, fumbling about, trying to find her specs. In the far corner, her wand rack was on fire. There was smoke, there were flames and all the wands were burning. Just one, at the very end, was not yet alight.

Mum's fingers went flying, scrolling and sourcing, then she pointed her spellstick. "Abrakkida Rune," she shouted, and water flooded down from the ceiling and drenched the wand rack.

The flames died to a sizzle, the fire was over – but Grandma's wand rack was a charred smoking ruin.

And then, cowering, a windsniffer crept out from behind Grandma's bed.

A very guilty-looking windsniffer. . .

We have lots of windsniffers around Moaning Mountain, living in the caves. If you don't have them where you live, windsniffers are rodents. Big ones, about the size of a witchtoddler. Only not cute like witchtoddlers are – I think maybe it's the stubby tusks or the huge nostrils, or maybe it's all the bristles.

Windsniffers are talented hunters though. They use those huge nostrils to sniff at the wind. And they can get the scent of tiny grubbles in the ground up to two miles away.

Windsniffers are also fire-breathers.

"A windsniffer? In *this* house?" Mum screeched. "We do NOT have pets in this house! Especially not ugly pets. Fire-breathing pets!"

"This is not a *pet*, Kristabel," snorted Grandma. "This is a guard-sniffer, a ghoul hunter. And we must let it roam the grounds!"

Yes. Grandma had decided that if a windsniffer can sniff out tiny grubbles two miles away, then maybe it could sniff out large ghouls in our garden.

"I have four words only to say to you," Mum hissed, right in Grandma's face. "GET! RID! OF! IT!"

And off she swirled.

I felt sorry for the windsniffer, cowering in the corner. And sorry for Grandma, who was cradling her wands – what was left of them – and looking miserable.

"Grandma, you've still got that one," I said, pointing to the wand tucked up in a little basket by her bed. "And this one."

I held out the only wand left in the ruins of the wand rack, the wand at the end. Short and stubby, pale whitish-grey in colour.

Grandma gave a snort. "That one," she said. "Troublesome. Useless. I only keep it because it was a gift."

Then she grabbed it off me. "See here," she said to the wand. "You and me. We'll NEVER get on. But for now, you are my only spare. So I am *stuck* with you."

Now I started to feel sorry for the wand.

"Grandma," I said. "Do wands understand witches?"

"They do," Grandma said. "Wands are living things, Flo, made with wood from the Enchanted Glades. And that one is a *menace*. A jiggler. A fidget."

"Maybe it would be less of a menace if you didn't shout at it," I said.

Because there's a witchboy in my class who jiggles and fidgets. A LOT. And all the witchteachers call *him* a menace. They all shout at him for jiggling and fidgeting. Except one witchteacher – she never shouts at him, and she gives him thirty seconds' jiggle-and-fidget-time every ten minutes. And she can get him to do anything.

Grandma snorted. "No, Flo," she said. "A wand like this only understands one thing. Firmness, and a good tight grip. Nasty little thing. Faulty, in my opinion."

Then she pointed at the wand tucked up in the basket. The long black one she uses most of the time. "THAT, Flo," she said, eyes gleaming. "*That* is the wand to use against a ghoul attack!"

A ghoul attack.

Not *again*.

"Grandma," I said. "Ghouls could NOT survive a magiquake."

"Ghouls certainly could, Flo," said Grandma firmly. "Ghouls came from underground – were sent back underground. Who knows what tunnels, what pathways, what skills ghouls have to survive underground?"

"But … they couldn't survive a thousand years," I said.

"Ghouls thrive in heat, Flo," said Grandma. "Ghouls gather strength from flames. And where better and hotter than the fiery centre of the witchglobe?"

"Well, if they thrive there, why do they come out at all?" I said.

"Because the urge to feed on witches grows too strong to ignore," said Grandma. Then she looked at me, eyes popping.

"Ghouls are strange and mysterious creatures, Flo," she said. "And the witchglobe is a strange and mysterious place – as strange on the inside as it is on the outside. *Anything* is possible."

"But, Grandma," I said. "No other witches think ghouls are on their way."

Grandma just glared at me. "I knew Kristabel would not listen to me," she said. "I thought Hetty would not listen to me. But you, Flo, I hoped you *would* listen to me."

Then she glared more. "Just because I am eighty-three years of age does NOT make me a silly old fool," she snapped.

✷

I tell you, I was glad to go to school.

Except, in the very first lesson – witchcitizenship – me, Lily and Kika were meant to draw a family tree showing all the Esteemed Graciouswitches currently living at Hovelhagg Palace. But did Lily and Kika help? No. They were too busy whispering about page 48 of the Book, and which of us would be best at handling sudden stardom. So I had to draw it alone.

Then they spent the whole of break time doing a quiz to find out what their witchgirl style was – page 14.

And at lunchtime they dawdled in the queue so long, discussing which were the healthy options for a witchgirl who was banishing bad eating habits – page 83 – that I'd finished my lunch before they even got to the table.

So I was glad to go home again.

Until I found Grandma in the kitchen, bottling her doppel potion. Her ghoul-fighting doppel potion.

Chapter 14

I *had* to ask. Had to know. "Grandma," I said. "How exactly is that doppel potion going to help your fight against ghouls?"

"Three drops and I shall turn myself into a ghoul!" Grandma said proudly. "Be as ghastly as any of them!"

Grandma? Turn herself into a *ghoul*? Why? Why would Grandma want to be a ghoul? Even if they *did* exist. Which they didn't, not any more.

So I asked her.

"But – why do you want to be a ghoul, Grandma?" I said.

"To seek out the swarm, find their lair, become one of them," said Grandma.

More questions were tumbling about in my head now. So many questions, I did NOT know which to ask first.

"But if you want to be a ghoul, Grandma," I said, "you can just do a transforming spell."

"No, no, no," said Grandma impatiently. "A transforming spell, Flo, that's the *look* of a ghoul. Good enough to fool other creatures. But not ghouls themselves."

Then she wagged a finger in my face. "To fool ghouls themselves there is only one way. Doppel potion," she said. "Because doppel potion – it *is* the creature!"

"So, tell me again," I said, trying – really trying – to understand Grandma's plan. "What will you do once you're a ghoul?"

"I shall join the swarm," said Grandma, eyes gleaming.

"But how will you find the swarm?" I said, more baffled than ever.

"A ghoul will be able to smell its own kind," Grandma said confidently.

"And once you've smelled them, found them, joined the swarm," I said. "What then?"

"I shall *lure* the ghastly creatures!" said Grandma.

Now, this was tricky. The more questions I asked, the less I understood. "*Lure* them?" I said.

"Lure them to their next ghoul attack!" said Grandma. "Lure them using fluent Ghoulish – which I shall speak, being a ghoul. Lure them to a place full of witchchildren!"

I gaped at Grandma. I couldn't help it. I was amazed by what was going on inside her head. "And … what place will you lure them to?" I said.

"The witchchildren's section of Haggspit Library!" said Grandma triumphantly.

Now, this was where I started to worry.

Because I am used to Grandma behaving strangely, but not *this* strangely.

And sometimes, if witches, especially old witches, start behaving strangely, it means they're not well, and need a potion.

Like Lily's great-auntie, who lives with Lily.

Because one day Lily's great-auntie decided Lily's mum was an evil serpent. One who had taken over Lily's mum's shape – and that the real Lily's mum was shackled to a big hook in its lair. And Lily's great-auntie kept setting up serpent traps, and refusing dinner that was cooked by a serpent. Then she started hiding in the bathroom cupboard to see if Lily's mum would transform into her evil serpent shape behind a locked bathroom door.

The witchmedics said Lily's great-auntie had Confusions. And now she's taking unconfusing potion, she's a lot better. Now she only occasionally thinks Lily's mum is an evil serpent.

So ... was that happening to Grandma? Confusions?

It seemed likely.

Because Grandma was confused enough to think Plucky was NOT a pixie – when he clearly *was*. Confused enough to think ghouls were NOT extinct – when they clearly *were*.

Oh dear. *Poor* Grandma.

It was probably best to go along with her Confusions, until Mum could make her an appointment to see a witchmedic.

"Grandma," I said carefully. "Haggspit Library sounds a very good luring plan..."

Although I didn't really think it was, because Haggspit Library is closing – or Merging, as the government calls it – in two weeks. So the ghoul attack would have to be before the government's Merging shut the library.

"But what then, Grandma?" I said. "Once your

ghouls are lured to Haggspit Library?"

"Then . . . an ambush!" said Grandma with a fierce light in her eyes. "We will ambush the ghastly creatures – thousands and thousands of witches, all doing one spell – and destroy them!"

Well, of course we would.

"And what spell will we do?" I said.

"There are small details of my plan, Flo," Grandma said, "that I still have to work on. Such as that spell."

Then she frowned and jabbed a finger at me. "Because ghouls, Flo, can survive almost *anything*," she said. "Those unlucky witches in the Great Ghoul War tried everything. Flaming spells just made the ghouls grow stronger; dissolving spells did *nothing*. And ten witches doing a shrinking spell on just one ghoul shrunk it by less than TWO CENTIMETRES – for under *ten seconds!*"

Then Grandma pulled herself up to her full height and looked me in the eye. "However, Flo," she said. "My plan will be complete by the time it is needed. I shall find the weak spot."

"The weak spot?" I said.

"All creatures have a weak spot – even ghouls," said Grandma, nodding more. "Mergrindles die of fright if they see their reflection. Snidlegreeps can

92

be tickled to death. Thrumbulgers dissolve in water. Once I am a ghoul, I shall think like a ghoul, act like a ghoul, know about ghouls – and the weak spot will become clear. So too will the spell."

Oh. Oh dear.

Poor *poor* Grandma.

Chapter 15

Poor Grandma. I read her ghoul booklet that evening.

GHOUL ATTACK: THE FACTS

Witchchildren - YOU are in most danger. Ghouls are cunning, cruel and lazy. During a ghoul attack, ghouls will go for the easiest target. This is NEARLY ALWAYS the smallest witches in any group.

Witchworld

Ghouls roam the witchglobe in search of food - witches. A witchvictim will transform into a ghoul within two minutes of a ghoul attack. The smaller the witch, the harder and more painful the transformation (see below) to ghoul.

Ghouls exist ONLY to attack. It is impossible for a small witchvictim - no matter how adorable or cute - to reason with a ghoul, or to beg and plead for mercy. A ghoul will take NO NOTICE.

Ghouls are attracted by NOISE. The gurgles of witchbabies, the happy shouts of witchchildren, the piercing shrieks of witchteens - particularly witchgirls - are like a DINNER BELL to a ghoul.

Ghouls are also attracted by LIGHT. Bright lights, flashing lights, any lights at all.

A hungry ghoul – and most of them are – will attack TWICE a day. This is once every twelve hours.

Twelve hours after a ghoul attack, the witchvictim – now all ghoul, the memory of its former life as a witchchild wiped out – will also be ready to carry out a ghoul attack. Also twice a day.
This means that, in ten days just ONE ghoul will become over ONE MILLION ghouls. See chart below.

Attacks	Total	Ghouls
Day 1	2	4
Day 2	8	16
Day 3	32	64
Day 4	128	256
Day 5	512	1024
Day 6	2048	4096
Day 7	8192	16,384
Day 8	32,768	65,356
Day 9	131,072	262,144
Day 10	524,288	1,048,576

It also means that in less than two

weeks the whole of Haggspit will be ghouls – including YOU.

GHOUL SWARMS

Ghouls hunt in swarms. When a swarm gets too large – around fifty ghouls – the swarm divides. This creates two new swarms. These swarms will continue to feed and divide until there are no witchvictims left. At this point, the whole of Witchworld – certainly everywhere below the Iceline – will be ghouls.

Warning signs that a swarm is near include:
smaller creatures scuttling for cover
a sudden drop in air temperature
foul smells
the sound of flapping wings
low growls and hisses

Any witchchild noticing two or more of the above should take cover. It is almost certain there is a ghoul swarm

within FIFTY METRES.
And remember – no NOISE and no LIGHTS. Do NOTHING to attract a ghoul's attention.

ATTACK METHOD

1) Gassing: A ghoul will first gas a witchchild with its foul breath.

2) Fatal biters: The attacking ghoul will then use its fatal biters on the unconscious witchvictim. It is usual for a standard ghoul to take three to four large bites out of a witchchild before feeling full.

3) Transformation: The agonising change from witchchild to ghoul takes approximately two minutes. The witchchild will be awake throughout.

SELF-DEFENCE MOVES

Last-Chance Lunge
Run-for-it Roll

Jawline Jab
Desperation Dodge

WARNING!!!
Witchchildren,
please note
the following.

These self-defence moves may offer you a small - extremely small - chance of escape against a standard ghoul.

However, there are also ROGUE GHOULS.

These rare ghouls are bigger, stronger, cleverer. They may have extra features, such as tusks or spikes or poison squirters. They hunt alone - and NO self-defence moves will help you. NO chance of escape is possible. NONE.

Beware a rogue ghoul.
This is the WORST
GHOUL OF ALL.

Yes. I read Grandma's booklet – then I chucked it in the bin. Because it was lacking one basic fact.

Ghouls were extinct…

But, all the same, I was worried for Grandma. It must be horrible being so sure ghouls were on their way. Poor Grandma.

But Grandma was not the only thing worrying me that evening. Because tomorrow was Wednesday. The day I had been dreading for weeks and weeks…

So I went to see Hetty.

Chapter 16

I stood outside Hetty's door, which is opposite mine … and shut. Of course.

Hetty says witchteens NEVER leave their bedroom door open, only teenies like me.

And well, yes, I *do* leave my door open. I keep hoping Hetty will see it's open and come in, like she used to.

But she hardly ever does. Not now.

I knocked, and I waited. Because that's the rule with witchteens, Hetty says.

"Enter," Hetty trilled, which was a good start. Because quite often when I knock and wait, Hetty screeches at me about witchteens needing privacy, and to go find a creepy little pixie to play with.

But not today. Today Hetty had Shriek Sistaz thudding out and she was standing in front of her mirror, making some weird shapes – which I think were dance moves – and trying on her Prom outfit. Again.

"Flo," she said happily, giving me a little twirl and taking a picture of herself on her skychatter. "I will *definitely* get a boyfriend wearing this."

Well, I wasn't so sure.

Hetty's robe was extremely tight, and extremely purple. A thin black serpent was knotted round her middle, hissing, and not looking at all like it was enjoying being a belt. Her tights were bright blue, her shoes were bright green and she was holding a bright-yellow bag – tiny and with no space to fit anything useful in it, like a pixie-spotting guide.

"Colour blocking," Hetty said proudly. "Living accessories and a cute clutch. Three trends nailed in one outfit."

I had no idea what Hetty was talking about, but then I often don't. Anyway, I had something to say.

"Hetty," I said. "I need advice—"

But just then there was a beep from Hetty's witchfixer and she held up her hand. "One moment, please," she said. "Kwikpik coming in."

A picture came up on screen. Hetty's friend Gigi, pouting like a fish and bulging her eyes. And some text: My freaky fish face.

Hetty snorted. Then she pointed her skychatter at me. "Do something funny," she ordered. "Do this." Then she stretched her mouth right out, bared all her teeth and lolled her head to one side.

"Hetty, listen to me," I said. "I don't want to go to Harridan's."

Hetty's head shot up. Her mouth dropped open. She let out a screech of laughter, then she stopped. "That is because you are seriously weird," she explained. "That is because of the Accident."

Oh no. Not the Accident *again*. Every time I don't think like Hetty – which is most days – she blames it on the Accident.

I was almost two when the Accident happened. I was outside, playing, when a skragglehead swooped down, bit me on the leg and hurled me across the garden. I landed hard. On my head.

It's one of the very few things that gets Mum dabbing her eyes. "Darling," Mum says. "We thought we'd lose you."

Because, as you may know, there's only one cure for a skragglehead bite. Restoring potion – the last-chance potion.

Mum showed me a picture. The toddler-me lying in a big white bed with witchmedics all around, restoring potion being dripped from a bottle through a tube into my arm.

"I sat by your bed," Mum says, sniffing. "I watched the potion bottle emptying, and I watched you. It was the worst few hours of my life."

I woke up twelve minutes before the restoring potion was all gone – and if I hadn't, that would have been it. No more me.

But Hetty always says that the Accident – being dropped on my head – jiggled my brain about, and that the restoring potion didn't mend it properly, and that's why I'm weird.

Like now, about Harridan's.

Harridan College. Expensive, select, packed with the daughters of celebrities, and in the top ten for witchsit results.

Harridan College. The upper school Mum wants me to go to next year. A school I do NOT want to go to, because I want to go to Chantings – which is just down the road.

But Mum starts to tremble when I mention Chantings. "Darling," she says. "Don't be silly. Ordinary witchgirls go to that school."

My point exactly.

And tomorrow — Wednesday — was the Harridan's Open Day. Me and three hundred other witchgirls, all looking round, sitting tests, doing interviews. Three hundred witchgirls all wanting a place there. And me.

With not even Lily and Kika for company, because Lily and Kika were looking round Covens.

"Hetty, I said. "I won't fit in at Harridan's. I know I won't. Look at me."

Hetty *did* look. A frown came over her face. She went pale. "You are so right," she moaned.

Because Hetty already goes to Harridan's — and she loves it. She started chewing her lip and panicking. "I'll be known as the witchteen with the freak for a sister!" she said. "The sister who doesn't own one single pair of lacy leggings! The sister who would rather save forest pixies than go to a Shriek Sistaz gig!"

She leaned forward and grabbed my hand. "OK, you *have* to fail. In the interview tell them your hobby is setting schools on fire."

"I can't," I said. "You know I can't."

Hetty made an exasperated sort of noise. "Flo," she said. "You will NEVER be a success as a witchteen if you don't learn how to lie. Life as a witchteen

106

depends on the ability to lie."

"But I just *can't*," I said. "I'm useless at it."

Which is true. Hetty's been trying to teach me for years.

"Hm," said Hetty, thinking hard now. "Here's what you do. On the tour you'll pass the ogre cage. It's padlocked and they think we don't know the combination, but we do – it's 2130. So let it out."

Then she got a piece of paper. She scribbled three words on it. "When you do the describing bit in the Ancient Witchspeak test, stick these in somewhere," she said, snorting with laughter. "That'll really get you in trouble. And answer everything wrong in the General Magic test."

Then she had another thought. "And I'll be in Hurlstruk House, so do something interesting there. Set the fire alarm off. Start a fight. Make a disgrace of yourself, so I can enjoy it."

She looked at me. She tutted. "Although you won't," she said, shaking her head sadly. "You just won't."

Then she waved me away. "Now go," she said. "There is less than one week until my Prom. Which means I have *stuff* to do."

Chapter 17

I tried. I really tried at Harridan's the next day to do what Hetty said – but I couldn't do it. I just could NOT cheat. Here is page one of my General Magic test.

SECTION 1: MAGIC KNOWLEDGE

Name any three sources of magic energy
The rocks of the Shivergrim Magic Mines
The Sleeping Serpent of Tark
The Enchanted Glades of Frakkenwild

Complete the following sentences

One unit of magic energy is known as a zapp

One hundred units of magic energy are known as a hexon

One thousand units of magic energy are known as a jinx

Give the two identity checks your spellstick does before it will work.

It checks your fingerprint.

It checks your voice.

Give two situations where your spellstick may need extra proof of identity.

When you have a cut finger or a blister, and your spellstick doesn't recognise your fingerprint.

When you have a cold, and your spellstick doesn't recognise your voice.

Give the main reason why spellsticks now use identity checks.

Because older witchchildren used to steal spellsticks from younger witchchildren, but now they don't because a spellstick won't work for the thief.

Is the sentence below true or false?
An under-twelve spellstick used outside the classroom will explode. True

What is a WIN number?
A WIN number is a Witch Identification Number. A four-digit number.

What must a witch do to get a WIN number?
A witch must send her wand and a fingerprint sample to the DWWS, which is the short name for the Department of Witch Wellbeing and Safety.

What is the purpose of a WIN number?
The DWWS connects the fingerprint of that witch to the wand, then issues a WIN number. Once the wand has a WIN number, it will only work if that witch is holding it.

How many years has it been the law that wands must have WIN numbers?
Seven.

Name one danger in using a wand. And explain what it is.
One danger is backsurge. This is when a wand

reverses the magic units back down the wand. Then, as well as doing the witch's spell, it does a spell on the witch.

I know. I know. One hundred per cent correct.

And I didn't stick the words Hetty gave me into my Ancient Witchspeak test. I even did the extra questions at the end for witchgirls who had time.

Then, when they asked me about hobbies in the interview, I said I like reading and painting.

As for the ogre cage – I walked straight past it.

I am a *fool*.

Then it got worse. Because at lunchtime all the witchgirls had to sit at big, long tables and talk to each other.

This is who was on my left.

Mimosa Shreek, sister of Zoe Shreek – witchscreen star and also a Harridan's old girl.

And on my right…

Tempest Triggstek, whose mum owns three magic mines in Shivergrim.

Tempest Triggstek took one look at me and gasped. "I know who you are," she said. And I knew what she was going to say next. The thing I hate witchkids saying.

She did.

"You're Tragic Flo," she said.

Yes. I *am* Tragic Flo. I am the famous Tragic Flo – well, famous in South Witchenland, at least. And, believe me, it's not a good thing to be famous for.

I was headline news for weeks and weeks and weeks.

TRAGIC FLO SEES MYSTERY BEAST TAKE DAD!
WHAT WERE GIANT CLAWS TRAGIC FLO SAW?

That's me. Tragic Flo.

Florence Skritchett.

Daughter of Lyle Skritchett, prize-winning witchscreen presenter and journalist – known and loved by witchkids all over South Witchenland.

Lyle Skritchett. Famous for *Stuff*. The show that brought witchkids news of a singing, juggling giant squid spotted in Kronebay, and vital facts like how many minutes a year a witchkid spends picking its nose in class.

Famous for *Beat That!* The show that got witchkids doing challenges against grown-ups – eating doughballs off sticks while being tickled by goblins, knitting a scarf out of serpents while rolling down a hill inside a giant ball…

Famous for being gone.

And for having a daughter, Tragic Flo.

Tragic Flo, who saw how it all happened, but who can't remember.

Tragic Flo, who witchmedics said suffered the Shocks. Such severe Shocks that she didn't speak for weeks and weeks. Shocks that mean, even now, she still sometimes wakes screaming from her sleep.

Tragic Flo, who doesn't want to even think about how it all happened.

So I don't. I block out the memory.

It's best that way.

Mum says I *should* think about it. She sits me down and pats my hand. "Darling," she says. "You must let yourself think about that dreadful evening. What you saw. What you felt. You must face your fears. Tell us what happened."

Well, maybe that's what I *should* do.

But I can't.

I am NOT thinking about the Claws. I'm just not. Anyway, my brain won't let me. It's too scary.

Because I can remember – clear as clear – the evening it all happened. The night the Ice Volcano got voted Seventh Wonder of Witchworld.

Me and Dad were there, up in the far north of Witchenwild, because of Dad's work. Out in the big hotel garden, wrapped up in big coats, watching fireworks going off everywhere, celebrating the win.

I remember the Ice Volcano erupting above us. Towering up, blasting great blizzards of ice high in the sky.

I remember Dad's hand in mine. "The Seven Wonders of Witchworld," he said. "You and me, Flo – one day we'll see them all. One day. I promise."

I remember Dad setting up a rocket in the garden then turning to me with a grin on his face. "I declare Florence Skritchett the Eighth Wonder of Witchworld," he said.

I remember Dad with his spellstick out, ready to light the rocket. And up in the sky, a burst of fireworks that lit up all the bushes, all the ground behind Dad.

And that's when I saw them.

The Claws.

Huge hooked Claws. Claws for scratching, for tearing, for ripping at things. Claws coming right out of the ground.

But that's it. That's where my memory stops.

The next thing I remember is being curled up

on the ground in a tight, tight ball. And torches beaming down the garden, and voices, and being wrapped in a big silver blanket and brought back up into the hotel.

And Dad was gone. Which is why they call me Tragic Flo.

But the thing is this. I'm *not* Tragic Flo.

I'm Sad Flo – of course I am. Sometimes so sad I actually ache. And I miss Dad all the time, especially weekends and holidays and birthdays.

And I'm quite often Fed-up Flo. Because I have a mum who has more fun with a daughter who likes shopping than with a daughter who likes forest pixies. And I have a sister who used to mostly do things with me but now mostly does things with witchteens.

But I am NOT tragic. Because Dad made a promise. That me and him, one day, we'll see all the Wonders of Witchworld. And Dad has never broken a promise to me. Not ever.

So I know – however long it takes, Dad will be back.

He *will*.

Chapter 18

I didn't think the day could get much worse, but it did. Because something happened on the tour. Something truly terrifying.

The tour started in Harridan Hall, which was big and old and dark. Then the tour wound through the Blocks – three buildings, still big but less old, less dark – and the Frivolities Hub, and the Potions Lab, and some other buildings whose names I can't remember.

After that the tour went outside, into the gardens. Past playing fields and gripball courts, past a lake with a merteacher bellowing instructions at splashing witchgirls, past a unicorn meadow.

Then it was the last stop on the tour. The newest building of all. All on its own, surrounded by trees.

A big oblong building, perched on a slope. Mainly glass, with big glass windows, lots and lots of them – and huge open glass doors, with wide stone steps sweeping up towards them.

Hurlstruk House.

Newly opened. Used for plays, concerts, art shows and special events. Named after Meristo Hurlstruk, who paid for it.

I trudged after Mum, and the tour. Trudged along the path. Up the stone steps. Across the stone terrace. In through the big glass doors.

And *that* was when the terrifying thing happened.

As soon as I set foot inside Hurlstruk House it happened. As soon as I looked round the big hall. At the huge stage, at the spotlights – and at Hetty.

Because Hetty was there, with a whole lot of witchteens. All busy putting up bunting, and streamers, and big sparkly banners. Preparing it for Prom night.

It was a feeling. A squirming, slithering feeling. One that started in my middle and crept through every bit of me.

A feeling I tried – at first – to ignore.

But I couldn't ignore it. Just *couldn't*.

It was a terrifying feeling. A feeling that got worse. Worse and worse and worse. Until it was so terrifying, so horrifying – it made me shudder. Actually shudder.

I shuddered and shuddered and shuddered. And once I started shuddering, I could NOT stop.

Because I started seeing things. Pictures. Scenes. Glimpses of things. Things that flashed past my eyes so fast I could hardly see them. Thing after thing after thing.

Scary things. Confusing things. Terrifying things.

Creeping, leaping shapes. Sharp teeth. Yellow eyes. Flashing lights. Flailing arms. Screaming mouths. And skyriders, and witches – and twisted white shapes in a black, black sky...

Thing after thing after thing. All so fast, so confusing, I could NOT slow them down. But I knew this. That if I *could* stop those things, slow them down, really look at them, then those pictures, those scenes, those glimpses – they would be showing me terrible, *terrible* things.

And there were sounds. Terrible sounds. Sounds of snarling, of growling, of hissing, of thudding. Sounds of screaming – terrified screaming. And one sound more terrible, more horrifying than *all* the others. A loud snarling noise, menacing and dangerous and EVIL.

So I stood there – and shuddered. I shuddered and shuddered and shuddered. And I could hear witchkids around me starting to gape, starting to giggle, but I still couldn't stop. Not the shudders. Not the pictures. Not the sounds.

Even when Mum turned round. Even when she stepped towards me, still, I could NOT stop.

Then I got a glimpse of eyes – vicious yellow eyes. Of huge green arms reaching out…

And I screamed. Really screamed.

As – BAM – I fell to the ground.

Mum was furious. Thought I was faking. She dragged me off the floor and on to my feet.

"I apologise for my daughter's ludicrous antics," she said stiffly to the teacher in charge of our tour. "I hope this will in no way affect her chances of a place in your excellent school."

The teacher just looked at Mum, sniffed and put a big cross against my name on the register.

Mum dragged me off to the skyshredder – but not before I saw Hetty grinning and giving me a thumbs-up from the far side of the room.

Mum shoved me in the flexipod and started the

engine.

"Florence Skritchett," she hissed, strapping herself in and glaring at me. "I am ashamed of you. You may not want to go to Harridan's, but that – whatever that was – was a VERY silly way to go about things."

"But, Mum," I said. "I couldn't help it. I saw things, lots of things. Scary things. Terrible things. And my whole insides they, well, they sort of – *shuddered.*"

Smoke shot out of both Mum's ears when I said that, but I had no idea why. She started hissing. Hard. Then she looked at me, eyes narrowed. "Shuddered?" she hissed. "Did you say *shuddered?*"

"Yes," I said, confused. Because for some reason, saying shuddered had got Mum even crosser. "And—"

Mum glared at me and ground her teeth. "NOT ANOTHER WORD!" she screeched right in my face.

Then she stamped her foot down and we took off.

It's best to do as Mum says when she's in that sort of mood. So I sat, silent and baffled, watching her break the speed limit all the way home.

✦

It's not nice when your grown-ups have a whole conversation in front of you that you don't understand.

But that's what happened to me when we got home.

Mum parked the skyshredder in the garage and dragged me through the back door. Grandma was in the kitchen, watching the news on the witchscreen – and strapping a pair of goggles the size of saucers across her face.

"You!" Mum hissed, snapping Grandma's goggles off, dumping them on the worktop and glaring at her. "You put Flo up to this. I know you did!"

"Kristabel," said Grandma calmly. "I don't have the foggiest idea what you're talking about."

"You wicked old witch," Mum shrieked. "You planned this! You NEVER liked Harridan's! You told Flo to *ruin* her chances of going there. You told her to pretend to be a Shudderer!"

"A Shudderer?" said Grandma, furious. "I most certainly did NOT."

Then she turned to me. "Flo," she said. "Did you pretend to be a Shudderer?"

"I don't even know what a Shudderer is," I said, feeling miserable and grumpy. "All I know is I got peculiar feelings. I saw things flashing in front of my eyes. Pictures. Scenes. Scary stuff. And I felt all shuddery."

"Well, well, well," Grandma said, looking proud of me. "Who'd have thought it? Little Flo, a Shudderer! Just like Mummy!"

A Shudderer… Just like Great-Grandma… What was Grandma talking about?

Mum marched over and glared right in Grandma's face. "We do NOT mention Shuddering in this house!" she hissed.

"Kristabel," snorted Grandma. "Why on earth not? You know perfectly well that Mummy was a Shudderer!"

"She was *ill!* She was a very Confused witch!" screeched Mum.

"She was NOT ill," said Grandma firmly. "She was a genius. An extraordinary phenomenon."

Then Mum turned on me. "As for you, Flo!" she shrieked, right in my face. "I expect *better* from you! You and your *ridiculous* plan! Pretending to Shudder! You have just destroyed – DESTROYED – your chance of a place at the finest school for witchgirls in South Witchenland!"

I stood there – feeling utterly baffled.

"Kristabel," said Grandma calmly. "Stop shrieking at poor Flo. There was NO ridiculous plan. It appears

122

that Flo has inherited the great gift of Shuddering from Mummy."

"Shuddering? A great gift? Hah!" shrieked Mum. "Whatever your mother had, it was NOT a great gift! It was some ghastly form of Confusions. Your mother was an embarrassment! An attention seeker! She brought shame on the Skritchett family name!"

Grandma snorted. "Only because witches were *too silly* to believe her Shudders!" she said.

It was all too much for Mum.

She gave a wail, then I watched — more baffled than ever — as she stamped her way out of the kitchen in a trail of smoke, across the hallway and into her office, then slammed the door shut.

Chapter 19

"Grandma, I don't understand," I said. "About me. About Great-Grandma. About Shuddering. Any of it. What *is* Shuddering? And why is Mum saying Great-Grandma had Confusions?"

"Because, Flo, your mother is *wrong*," said Grandma firmly. "Mummy was NOT ill, or Confused."

Grandma leaned forward. "Shuddering, Flo," she said, looking proud, "is the gift of seeing witchhistory!"

Witchhistory? Was *that* what I saw?

"It is a great gift to Shudder, Flo," said Grandma, eyes gleaming. "To see events from our past. Things that happened – sometimes long, long ago – right there, on that very spot. Ghastly, gruesome events, most of them. Brutal battles for survival!"

Oh… I was not at all sure I wanted the great gift of Shuddering.

"So, Flo, tell me," said Grandma, clasping my hand. "What did you see? What astonishing scenes from witchhistory came alive in front of your eyes?"

"I don't know *what* I saw, or what astonishing scenes they were, Grandma," I said. "There were creeping things, leaping things, lots of scary eyes and sharp teeth, and LOTS of screaming – and twisted shapes in the sky. But it was all so fast. I couldn't slow it down. Couldn't really see."

"*That*, Flo, is because you are a beginner," Grandma said kindly. Then she patted my hand. "Things will become easier to see, just as they did with Mummy. Each Shudder grislier, gorier – clearer – than the one before!"

Which I think was meant to cheer me up. But it didn't.

Then Grandma's eyes gleamed. "Shuddering, Flo," she said, "is a great gift that belongs to only two witches in the whole of Witchworld. First Mummy, and now you. The first Skritchett inheritor of Shuddering!"

Inheriting... I know about inheriting, because Kika explained it to me.

Kika's family have green-haired inheriting. There was one green-haired Rorrit way back in witchhistory, and sometimes – not often – there is another green-haired Rorrit, which is the inheriting. And last month a Rorrit witchbaby, Kika's new sister, was born with lots of fluffy green hair. The first green-haired inheriter for almost one hundred years.

But was Grandma right? Did Great-Grandma really Shudder? Mum didn't think so.

"Grandma," I said. "Why does Mum think Great-Grandma was ill? Confused?"

"Because, Flo, of Mummy's very first Shudder," said Grandma. "The first bit of witchhistory she saw – at the age of only eleven!"

"What did she see, Grandma?" I said.

"The Deadly Dodger Attack on Drool!" Grandma said proudly.

Oh. The Deadly Dodger Attack.

Famous – as every single witchkid in the whole of United Witchenlands knows. But not as witchhistory...

As a *myth*.

"Grandma," I said. "The Deadly Dodger Attack

didn't actually happen. It was a myth. A made-up story. In *Magical Myths of the Witchenlands*."

"It was NOT a myth," said Grandma firmly. "It is witchhistory."

But just then Grandma sat bolt upright and stared at the witchscreen.

"Look! Look!" she said, leaning forward and pointing. "There! The pelloligans. They're *migrating!*"

It was breaking news. Just coming through on the witchscreen.

The pelloligans of Moaning Mountain – the thousands and thousands of them that nest in the Forest of Fears – were migrating. The whole flock was leaving the mountain, heading south to the Narrowlands for the winter. But six weeks earlier than usual.

Now, maybe that doesn't sound like big news to some of you witchkids – but, believe me, to us witchkids in Haggspit it *is* big news. Because the pelloligans *never* migrate early. The pelloligans migrate on the same day every year.

But not this year.

A witchboffin was being interviewed. Saying the migrating was probably because of the new magic masts on Moaning Mountain. The new ones, put up to stream extra magic supplies down to Haggspit, because witches are using up magic supplies faster and faster each year.

The witchboffin said the streaming was interfering with the pelloligans' brain waves. That the streaming was confusing their sense of time. And that's why they were migrating early.

It sounded likely to me. But not to Grandma. She just sat there shaking her head. "It's not magic masts," she said. "It's ghouls. Ghouls underground. Ghouls digging upwards. Ghouls on their way. Ghouls turning the air colder and colder. *That's* why the pelloligans are migrating."

No. Not again. Maybe it was time to say something.

Poor Grandma. Confused about the Deadly Dodger Attack – about myths, about witchhistory. And very, VERY confused about ghouls.

Ghouls…

"Grandma," I said – and I tried to choose my words carefully because I didn't want to upset her. "We do actually have *proof* ghouls are extinct."

Grandma snorted. "We do NOT, Flo," she said. "We have proof only that ghouls were swallowed by a magiquake."

"Grandma," I said, choosing my words even more carefully. "I know you really do *think* there are ghouls.

You think ghouls could survive a magiquake...
You think ghouls could live a thousand years
underground..."

Grandma turned to look at me. "And you *don't*
think that?" she said.

I shook my head. "No, Grandma," I said. "I don't.
And maybe, Grandma... Maybe you think there are
ghouls, that ghouls still exist because you're a little
bit ... not-well."

Grandma glared at me. "Do I *look* a little bit not-
well?" she snapped.

I couldn't help gulping. Because, no, Grandma
didn't look a little bit not-well. But she did look a
big bit not-happy.

Then she stood up, glaring at me more. "I am
perfectly well," she snapped. "And every single thing
I have told you is TRUE."

Then she marched off out of the kitchen.

Chapter 20

I sat in the kitchen, listening to Grandma's bedroom door shutting with a slam. Then I heard the *putt putt putt* of Hetty's skyscooter landing by the garage. And soon Hetty's beaming face appeared in the kitchen doorway.

She clacked over and gave me a little punch on the arm. "Nice work, little Flo," she said. "Pretending to Shudder! Genius!"

She beamed more.

"You show great promise," she said. "That was lying of the very first order. You may yet turn into a truly excellent witchteen liar."

"Hetty," I said. "All that Shuddering, the screaming, the falling over… It wasn't lying of the very first order – not that I'm sure what that is exactly – it was the truth."

Hetty cackled. "Still doing it! Still lying!"

Then she gave me this look which was part admiring, part astonished. "You know," she said. "I was beginning to think I might be the only witchteen in the whole of Witchworld who has a sister who really CANNOT lie."

"Hetty," I said. "I'm *not* lying. Not now. Not then."

Hetty's eyes started to narrow. "Hm," she said.

Then she peered right up close, nose to nose with me. "Say that again," she said, staring straight into my eyes.

"I am NOT lying," I said.

Hetty stood back, stuck her head on one side and stared at me. Carefully. "You know what? I believe you," she said slowly.

Then I heard Mum's office door opening.

"Hetty," I said, feeling glum. "Maybe you believe me – but Mum doesn't. She thinks I was faking those Shudders."

But then Mum came into the kitchen. "Flo," she said, pulling up a chair and sitting down. "I have realised something. This is *not* your sort of prank.

Hetty might pretend to have the Shudders, but not you. You really *can't* lie. You NEVER lie."

Now Mum was biting her lip. "Which means, I am sorry to say. . ." she said. "You may be showing signs of those same ghastly Confusions your great-grandmother suffered from."

She leaned forward and checked my forehead. "Not too hot, so no fever. That's good," she said. "And how do you feel? Any strange symptoms? Giddiness? Shaking?"

"Mum, I feel fine," I said.

"And fine, Flo, is how you will stay," said Mum firmly. "Because Great-Grandma would NOT accept any treatment. She ranted and raved, told witchhistorians to listen and learn from her Shudders. Leapt up in meetings, in lectures, wagging her finger and telling them of the missed opportunity to discover important things about witchhistory."

Mum gave my hand a pat. "But you, Flo, will be a sensible Skritchett," she said. "You will have the best treatment money can buy. We will see the finest witchmedics. We will *control* your Confusions."

Then she peered closely at me. Her eyebrows shot up. "Good gracious, Flo," she said. "You're quaking. Actually quaking."

Which I was. Because I couldn't help thinking

about all the things that I saw.

"Mum," I said. "Those things, those shapes, all the leaping and creeping, all the screaming, and those eyes, yellow eyes, terrified eyes – they scared me. They really did. And there was one noise – loud and snarling and evil – it scared me SO much."

"There is no need to be scared, Flo," said Mum firmly. "All that Shuddering you did, those things you saw, are signs of Confusions. Which can be treated – and caught this early will probably be *cured*."

"Kristabel," said Grandma's voice from the doorway. "You are right that Flo has no need to be scared. But NOT because the Shudders are signs of Confusions."

Then Grandma looked at me. "Flo," she said. "Everything you see with your Shudders – all those scenes, those glimpses, they are from the *past*. Gone. Witchhistory. And THAT is why you have no need to be scared."

Then Grandma glared at Mum and walked off.

✳

It took me a long time to get to sleep that night. Hours. Because it's horrible thinking you might have Confusions.

And anyway ... was Mum right? Did I have

Confusions? I wasn't sure. The things I saw did make me FEEL confused. But was that the same thing as actually having Confusions?

I just didn't know.

But I could NOT stop thinking about all those things – those terrible things – I saw in Hurlstruk House. How they made me shudder.

So I tossed, and I turned, and when I – finally – slept I had strange muddled dreams. Terrifying dreams.

Dreams of my Shudders. Dreams of things creeping, things leaping. Dreams of screams and of struggles. Dreams of witches and skyriders, and twisted shapes in the sky. Dreams of eyes, vicious yellow eyes, and arms reaching out to grab... And dreams of that terrible *terrible* noise...

And I woke, quaking still more. Because – even though Mum said I had no need to be scared... Even though Grandma said I had no need to be scared...

I WAS scared.

Very scared.

I just didn't know why.

Chapter 21

GRATED DRAGON'S TOOTH

DRIED TROLL TOENAILS

Mum was already in the kitchen on Thursday morning when I came in for breakfast. Swooping around, talking on her skychatter. "Miranda, my speech!" she was saying. "We must work on my speech. Conference must be dazzled. I need wit! I need grit! I need facts and figures."

Then she turned as I came in. "Flo," she said, swooping over and patting my hand. "I have made an appointment with the most senior witchmedic in Upper Haggspit Medicentre. We will see her next week. We will get answers. Solutions. Reassurance about your condition."

There was a snort from the doorway – and there was Grandma, scowling at Mum. "There IS no condition, Kristabel," she said. "Flo is no more Confused than I am."

"Mother," Mum said firmly. "I have also booked you an appointment for next week. I think it would be useful for you to have a check-up."

Grandma glared. "You think *I* have Confusions?" she said. "Well, I don't. Nor does Flo. Nor did Mummy. There is not one single Skritchett who has Confusions – except possibly YOU."

Then Grandma marched over and switched on the witchscreen. She hunched in a chair right in front of it and started watching the news. Then – "Hah!" she said, and turned the volume right up.

There was more breaking news…

This time, news of strange knocking noises on Moaning Mountain. And another witchboffin was being interviewed. Saying the knocking noises were most likely echoes from the drilling on the new Potions2Go building site.

"It's ghouls," said Grandma with a grim look on her face. "Ghouls digging, ghouls gouging their way out of the ground. Ghouls close to breaking through. That's what the noises are."

Mum came over and turned the volume right

down. "Mother," said Mum, and there was a pleading note in her voice now. "It is JUST a check-up, that is all. I would like to *know* you are well. This is an important time for me, for the magazine. I don't want to be worrying about you."

"It's not *me* you should be worrying about," said Grandma. "It's *ghouls*."

"Mother, I AM worrying about you," said Mum, trying her best to keep calm. "All I ask is you keep the appointment."

"Not going," said Grandma firmly. "I don't need an appointment. What I need is thousands of witches to stop being as silly as you are, and start believing me about ghouls."

Then she glared at Mum, and Mum heaved a sigh, then went to get ready for work.

I sat down next to Grandma, because I'd been thinking. A lot. Thinking this:

That I wanted Grandma to be right and Mum to be wrong.

Thinking that I would much rather Shudder, much rather see bits of witchhistory – however gory or gruesome – than have Confusions.

"Grandma," I said. "Tell me about Great-Grandma, about the Shudders. How was she the only witch in Witchworld – up to now – to Shudder? How is that possible? Was she born a Shudderer? Did something happen that turned her into a Shudderer?"

"Flo," said Grandma. "There are many things for you to know about Shuddering. And how your great-grandmother got the Shudders – *that* is quite a story. But GHOULS are now the most important thing. The Shudders will have to wait."

"But, Grandma," I said. "You said Great-Grandma saw the Deadly Dodger Attack. How could she? Why are you so sure that was *real?*"

"Because, Flo," said Grandma, "of a Blob."

Then she leapt up from the table. "But now is not the time to tell you about the Blob, Flo," she said firmly, pulling a big box off one of her shelves. "Now we must deal with ghouls."

"But I've got so many questions, Grandma," I said miserably. "There's so much I want to know."

Grandma looked at me. "And, Flo, you *will* know," she said. "But for now, know this. You do NOT have Confusions."

Then Grandma started pulling things out of the box. Bits of wood, wire, pegs, nails. A hammer. A saw...

And I knew straight away. Grandma was building some kind of ghoul trap.

Then the clock struck eight and I heard Mum

calling me. It was time for school.

✴

I saw Lily and Kika in the playground and ran over. "Saturday," I said. "Is it OK?"

Because yesterday Mum said Lily and Kika could sleep over while she was at Conference. So I called them last night – as I had plans for a sleepover *my* way, and not one of those plans involved the Book. But Lily and Kika said they had to check first. And neither of them had called back.

"Er…" said Lily, looking a bit shifty.

"Thing is…" said Kika.

And, no, it seemed it *wasn't* OK. There was a witchmum ban on Lily and Kika sleeping over on Saturday – the moment their witchmums found out that the only grown-up who'd be there was Grandma.

Because Grandma had been busy yesterday. Going door to door, talking to witches about the ghoul attack, about the immediate evacuation of all witchkids.

Lily's and Kika's mums had both had a visit.

✴

It got worse. In the afternoon we had a gripball match against a team from the other side of Haggspit Harbour. The side Grandma used to live on.

And after the match, the witchgirl who played Central for their team – a witchgirl I've never liked – started giggling in the changing rooms. "I've got something of your Grandma's," she said. Then she waved Grandma's ghoul booklet – the first one – in my face.

"Interesting reading," she said. Then she started reading aloud. "Witchchildren," she read as the rest of her team started giggling too. "YOU are in most danger. Ghouls are—"

I snatched the booklet off her and stuffed it in my school bag. I could feel my face burning, going bright green.

Then Lily stepped forward. "It so happens her grandma has a very TRAGIC RARE illness," said Lily. "And you should be ashamed of mocking an old witchlady who is in fact extremely likely to leave our world for the Great Cacklecloud in the sky in the next FEW WEEKS."

Then she marched over to stand next to me.

"And," said Kika, also marching over, "it is in fact a very CONTAGIOUS tragic rare illness. Which means you may have already got it simply by touching that booklet. If you find within the next four weeks you experience any strange symptoms, such as boils or trembling, go straight to Haggspit

Hospital, the emergency department."

Then they each linked an arm through mine and
we all walked off, with our noses stuck in the air.

Chapter 22

Back home after school, I went straight to my bedroom – because I've got a tank full of buzzfish on one wall, and they need a buzz every day.

I lifted the tank lid and out they shot.

Buzzfish are my favourites – and I've got four. Two girl buzzfish and two boy buzzfish. The girl buzzfish buzzed round my head, then nibbled on my ears. The boy buzzfish shot across the room and nibbled on the end of my bed. So I ran over to shoo them off, because of Mum. She gets fed up with all the teeth marks.

Then I heard Hetty coming back from school,

flinging the back door open and clack-clack-clacking through the house. She burst into my bedroom, eyes shining.

"I have news, Flo," she gasped, clutching my arm and dodging the smallest buzzfish – Anemone – who buzzed over to say hello.

"Gigi has almost got a *boyfriend!* She was on her skyscooter and she stopped at the filling station, but she couldn't get the cap off the dragon oil tank. And he's working there and he helped her! And they got talking – because he's got the exact same skyscooter – and he's asked her to go for a walk in Haggspit Park when he finishes work! At six!"

Then she stopped clutching my arm so she could clasp her hands together. "And – AND," she said. "He's got a friend! And I'm going for a walk too. With the friend!"

She stopped then – because she had no breath left. Then she beamed and rushed off to her bedroom, and I heard thuds, and clangs, and cupboard doors slamming open, then shut, then open again, and less than a minute later Hetty was back.

She had her hair piled up on her head like a big messy bird's nest, long scary fake eyelashes, and she was tottering on shoes with big stacked-up heels. NOT shoes to wear for a walk in the park, in my opinion.

"This is it, Flo," Hetty said – and I thought she might actually explode with excitement. "Fate! A good fate! An excellent fate!"

Oh. Fate again…

Hetty is always going on about fate – which, I think, is what Hetty calls the future. Going on about how there are hundreds of fates, different futures, waiting out there for a witchteen every day. Good fates, bad fates, thrilling fates.

Like today.

And Hetty wasn't finished about fate. "Flo," she said, eyes huge. "Today a *bad* fate – Gigi not getting the cap off her dragon oil tank – has turned into a *good* fate! For her! For me!"

She did the arm-clutch on me again. "And this fate, Flo, is the fate I have been waiting for *all* year. Imagine! I may not *need* to find a boyfriend at the Prom. I may already have one! An actual boyfriend! Me! Even BEFORE my Prom! Because of this fate!"

Then she grabbed my hands. "Flo!" she said. "Wish me luck. This could be True Love! At last! Back later!"

And she shot off out again.

✦

144

I let my buzzfish have quite a long buzz, then I put feed in the tank, so they all buzzed back in. I put the lid on and did my homework – three whole paragraphs about the Extraordinary Elemental Disaster of the Strikkenlands.

Doing homework always makes me hungry, so I went into the kitchen.

Grandma was already there, cooking up something in a big pot. "Pelloligan stroganoff," she said, smacking her lips. "Ready in one hour, Flo!"

One hour. Well, it was worth the wait. I like Grandma's pelloligan stroganoff. It's tasty. Much better than the ready-stroganoff Mum puts in the witchowave.

Then Mum swirled in, all dressed up and ready to go out – and just then the front door buzzer went.

Which meant Mum's new boyfriend was here. Micky Ratizzo…

Micky Ratizzo. Famous witchscreen actor – well, famous in United Witchenlands, but I don't know about other landzones.

Micky Ratizzo. Star of *Rivals*. And – in real life – just like the creepy witchcop he plays in *Rivals*. Only worse.

He's not True Love though.

Because Mum is not like Hetty. Mum doesn't

want True Love. Mum already tried True Love, with Dad. And True Love worked for a bit, then it didn't.

I was only three, so I don't remember much about it. Hetty does though. Even now she grinds her teeth when she talks – well, screeches – about it.

"I am totally damaged!" she screeches. "I should ring Witchkidline! Did I come home from school to the smell of baking? No! I came home to Spellstick Wars!"

That's what Hetty calls life with Mum and Dad when True Love stopped working. Spellstick Wars. She says Mum and Dad were always arguing, always having illegal spell fights. The sort of fights where Mum would turn herself into a wild dragon and chase Dad round the garden trying to set him on fire, and Dad would send Mum – in her dressing-robe and slippers – to the top of Moaning Mountain in a blizzard.

In the end Hetty got so fed up she stole their spellsticks. She got Grandma to do an imprisonment spell on Mum and Dad, and stick them in a cage full of two-headed grinthogs. And Hetty said she'd only get Grandma to undo the spell when they agreed to divorce.

Which they did.

So now Mum's quite clear. "No True Love

nonsense. Never EVER again," she says. "I want just three things in a boyfriend. "Money. Celebrity. And a good strong bumpy nose. Nothing more."

And sure enough, in Micky swaggered, all quiffy hair and dazzling smile.

Hetty reckons he's spent a fortune on Potions2Go for his teeth, and she's probably right. They're perfectly pointy, all matching yellow, and when he smiles little stars ting and shine all over them.

He shone his dazzling smile on me. "Florence," he said. "How are you?"

He didn't wait for a reply — he was too busy turning and flashing his dazzling smile at Grandma.

"And who have we here?" he said.

"That's my mother," said Mum wearily. "Dorabel."

"Dorabel," he said, grabbing Grandma's hand and kissing it. "Enchanted to meet you."

Then he swaggered back over to Mum, while Grandma made being-sick faces at me behind his back.

He held out a big bunch of spiky scarlet flowers. "For you, my dearest," he said as the flowers started singing a horrible song all about love.

Mum started making cooing, oohing noises, which I think meant she liked the flowers. Then she handed them to me. "Put these in water for me, darling," she said, tucking her arm through Micky's. And they headed for the door.

I heard the clunk of flexipod doors slamming shut, the roar of a skysniper taking off and they were gone.

Leaving just me and Grandma alone in the house.

Chapter 23

GRATED DRAGON'S TOOTH

DRIED TROLL TOENAILS

"Follow me, Flo," Grandma said. "We have work to do!"

So I followed her as she marched to her bedroom and grabbed a statue off her desk. An ugly statue. A stone gargoyle. Small and chunky and grinning, with fat puffy lips and knotted eyebrows.

Then I followed her again as she tucked the statue under one arm and marched back through the hallway, and into the sitting room.

Mum's sitting room is mainly white, with big cream sofas and a long glass wall looking out over all the views.

The other long wall is all white. One long white wall with nothing on it. Just what Mum calls a statement fireplace – a huge thing, made of glowing dark-orange stone with a glowing dark-orange mantelpiece above it.

And Grandma's gargoyle. Which she plonked in the middle of the mantelpiece.

"Grandma," I said. "Mum won't let that stay in here. You know she won't. She'll hate it."

"This, Flo, is not all it seems," Grandma said. Then she looked at me with a glint in her eye. "Remember Room Twenty-Three?"

Well, yes. I *did* remember Room Twenty-Three.

Room Twenty-Three of the Haggspit Museum of Witchhistory. Grandma took me there for my sixth birthday. It was full of tatty old things. An old slipper. A stuffed bat hanging upside down on a perch. A painting of a dragon. All with one thing in common.

Each one was disguising a magic mirror…

The sort that have been banned for the last twenty years.

"Grandma, they're *banned*," I said. "Against the law. You can't go peeping into other witches' houses. It's snooping."

"The government snoops," said Grandma.

"They've got those spycam thingies everywhere. There's one poking out of the tree right outside this house. If the government can snoop, then so can I."

"Spycams are to stop crime," I said.

"They're for snooping," Grandma said. "Seeing what witches are up to. Nosing about in witches' business."

"But, Grandma," I said. "If spycams really *can* see everywhere, they might be watching you right now. They'll see your magic mirror."

I was panicking a bit now. Because having a magic mirror is a serious bit of law-breaking. And I had no idea exactly what happened to witches who got caught with a magic mirror — but it wouldn't be good.

"They will *not* see the mirror," said Grandma. "A magic mirror is only visible to the witch who uses it, and those in the room with her — one of *many* useful features. Besides, I am NOT snooping. I am watching for ghouls."

Ghouls…

"Grandma," I said. "If there really *are* ghouls, then the spycams will see them. The government will do something about them."

Grandma shook her head. "The government would not believe in ghouls if one came and sat in on one of their silly meetings," she said. "If those spycams spot ghouls, the government will think it's a hoax. Witchpranksters at work. Those spycam pictures will go to fifteen government departments for analysis. Discussion. Meetings. By the time the government decide to act, it will be too late. We'll all be ghouls."

Then Grandma got out her wand.

"This magic mirror can show me the whole of Witchworld," she said. "Every mountain, every forest, every ocean. Every town, every street, every house."

She leaned forward. "But now, Flo, there is only one place we want to see."

Grandma gave the gargoyle a brisk tap with her wand. "*Abrakkida Parikk, Aggenti Spekkulik*," she said, waving her wand about. "*Onkaddik Onraddik Agune.*"

Something silver, something shiny, rippled through the statue. Rippled – slowly, slowly – from top to bottom, like a wave over sand. Rippled until the whole statue glowed silver.

Then it began to … well, *melt*.

It's the only word I can find. The only word to explain what I saw. The fat silver lips, the knotted silver eyebrows, the whole fat silver head, started melting.

Dripping and pooling and swirling slowly across the mantelpiece, making a thick silver puddle. A puddle of something – but I didn't know what. Something not quite a liquid, not quite a solid.

Something that grew. That swirled sideways. Swirled across the mantelpiece, down towards the floor, up towards the ceiling. Spreading slowly out and out and out – until it was one huge shimmering wall. A shimmering wall of silver mirror glass.

And completely blank…

For now.

"Magic mirror," Grandma said, speaking loudly and clearly, "show me the Forest of Fears. Show me the autumn trees."

Then she tapped the mirror three times with her wand.

The magic mirror glowed and filled the room with light. Bright light, strong and dazzling – like a sun had dropped out of the sky and landed right here, in the sitting room.

Then, there it was. The Forest of Fears. In the heart of Moaning Mountain – so big, so thick, that no witch has ever dared venture right into the middle.

I stared at the trees. Thousands of them, all with leaves quivering softly in the breeze. Early summer leaves. Fresh and young, soft shades of greens and blues.

Except for one clump of trees. A clump – as big as two or three gripball pitches – with leaves that were red and gold and orange. Autumn leaves, in the middle of summer. Just like Grandma said.

"The trees think autumn is here, that winter is approaching," said Grandma. "But it's not winter approaching … it's ghouls."

I stared at the magic mirror. At the Forest of Fears. At the autumn trees. I stared and stared and stared.

Chapter 24

"Goodnight, Grandma," I said, standing in the sitting-room doorway.

I was in my pyjamas now, ready for bed. It had NOT been a good evening. Whatever I did – reading, watching the witchscreen, learning Fangwegian spellings for Monday – my mind kept wandering. Back to Grandma. Back to the sitting room. Back to the magic mirror...

Back to the trees. The autumn trees.

"Goodnight, Flo," said Grandma, blowing me a kiss.

I turned to go – and there was a roaring sound

outside. The roar of a skycab landing in the front garden.

Seconds later, Mum swirled in through the front door and slammed it behind her. Then swirled across the hallway, hissing and grinding her teeth.

Oh. Mum's date had *not* gone well, that was clear.

"The two-timer!" Mum hissed, right in my face. "All this time, seeing me, seeing her – HER! The editor of *Scoop!* And now – NOW – he's dumped me! Tonight! Decided *she* is more glamorous, *she* is richer – and that *she* will give him more magazine coverage!"

Then Mum swirled straight into her office. She started thudding about, switching things on, rustling things. There was a shriek, and Mum swirled back out, waving a sheet of paper with lots of numbers on it.

"Look. Look!" she hissed. "Their circulation figures this week – trebled! All because of that Pop-up Pamper Party!"

She started slapping her head, and paced through the doorway into the sitting room. "I need new readers!" she said, eyes staring wildly at me, at Grandma, all around. "Better stories! Bigger circulation figures! How? *How?*"

Then she stopped. She gaped.

Mum had – *finally* – noticed the magic mirror.

I got ready to block my ears. I thought Mum would start screeching at Grandma about being an irresponsible old witch. About how, of all the laws Grandma had broken this year, having a banned magic mirror was the worst.

Mum didn't.

She raced over and clutched Grandma's arm. "Mother," she gasped. "This is the answer! I shall peer! Peek! Find out dark celebrity secrets! Break major celebrity scandals! Look in celebrity bathrooms! Celebrity kitchens! Celebrity holiday homes! The circulation figures will *rocket!*"

Grandma may be small, but she's terrifying when she wants to be – and she was now.

She stood and looked straight up at Mum. "Kristabel," she said. "I am *ashamed* of you. What a witch sees in her magic mirror stays in her magic mirror. It is CONFIDENTIAL."

"But, Mother," said Mum. "I *must* have more readers. I must do better than *Scoop!*"

Now Mum was pawing at Grandma's sleeve. "Mother, if you care about me, if you love me, you will HELP!"

Grandma shook her off and glared. "Help you,

Kristabel?" she said. "A magic mirror is NOT for snooping."

Mum flushed bright green and hung her head. "Sorry, Mother," she mumbled, and she was tugging at her fingers and chewing at her lip, and looking miserable. "It's just … well…"

Grandma glared more. "What did I teach you all those years ago, Kristabel?" she said. "All those years sitting at my knee? Did you not listen? Did NOTHING go in? The importance of honesty? Loyalty? Integrity among witches?"

Mum's head was completely down now.

"Not one story," said Grandma severely. "This magic mirror is in here for one reason and one reason only. Ghoul watching!"

Mum's head snapped up. Her mouth dropped open. "Ghoul watching?" she hissed.

"From now on, someone must watch it day and night. There is no telling when ghouls will arrive!" said Grandma.

"Help," shrieked Mum, staggering about. "Save us! Only weeks away!"

Then she clutched Grandma's arm. "How many ghouls, Mother? How many?"

"Hard to say," said Grandma, shaking her off. "Possibly two or three, possibly more."

"Two or three ghouls! Oh no!" shrieked Mum, doing more staggering. "Save us all from a huge, hideous ghoul attack!"

"Let me tell you a bit about ghouls, Kristabel," Grandma snapped. "Two or three ghouls is quite enough to turn every witch in Haggspit into a ghoul within days. Because within MINUTES, two ghouls will become four. Then four will become eight. And within DAYS two ghouls will become—"

"No more!" shrieked Mum. "You're scaring me! And when – *when* – will this terrifying attack be?"

"That I don't know," said Grandma. "Maybe a week. Maybe less. And *that*, Kristabel, is why—"

But Mum was already gone. Staggering back to her office, hissing and clutching her head and most definitely NOT happy at all.

Hetty was not happy either. The back door slammed and Hetty came clacking through the kitchen, across the hallway and into the sitting room.

Not hissing like Mum – but wailing.

"Fate can be so CRUEL," Hetty wailed. "Me and the witchboy went to the park, but so did Veracity. And he's asked her out, not me. Her! *Her!*"

Then Hetty flung herself on a chair. "It's the nose, I know it is!" she hissed. "You know how many bumps Veracity's nose has got? Three. *Three!*"

Then she sniffed. Whipped a small mirror out of her handbag and checked her reflection, peered into it. Peered at her nose from all angles – and her mouth started trembling again.

"Henrietta," said Grandma, throwing her a pair of very big goggles. "Try these on for size. Ghoul spit can blind a witch."

Hetty's mouth stopped wobbling. She gaped at Grandma.

"And I suggest flat shoes and loose robes at all times," Grandma said. "If ghouls attack you must be prepared to dodge and run."

Hetty stood up. She frowned. Hurled the goggles across the room. And marched off to her bedroom.

Chapter 25

All Friday in school, I thought.

I thought about me. All those glimpses, those scenes, those terrifying Shudders. I thought about Mum – so sure they were signs of Confusions. About Grandma – so sure they weren't.

And I wondered.

Mum… Grandma… Which of them was right?

I thought more. About the pelloligans migrating, all the knocking noises inside the mountain. About Grandma, staring into her magic mirror. About those trees. Those autumn trees…

I thought about Mum – so sure that ghouls were

extinct. About Grandma – so sure they were not.

And again, I wondered.

Mum… Grandma… Which of them was right?

But, for the very first time, I just wasn't sure of the answer.

And at lunchtime when Lily and Kika got the Book out I said I was going to the library because I wanted to read an actual book, one worth reading, instead.

But I didn't read. I sat and stared. Down at the floor, out of the window, up at the sky. And I thought more.

I thought about Dad. About what Dad said. And I could hear his voice in my head, clear as clear…

"Never laugh at the ways of old witches. Your grandmother knows more about spells, more about potions, more about Witchworld than most."

And I knew. Something inside me was beginning to change.

When I got home I went to see Hetty. Knocked on her door and went in.

Hetty was tipping a big bag of make-up out on her bed.

"Hetty," I said. "I need to talk to you."

"Brief, Flo, keep it brief," said Hetty. "Witchteen with Prom to prepare for. Important stuff only."

"Well, this is important to me," I said. "It's about ghouls. About a ghoul attack."

That made Hetty turn round. "A ghoul attack?" she said, cackling.

"Grandma seems really sure there *will* be one," I said. "Here. In Haggspit. And I just wondered if she might be—"

Hetty stopped cackling and gaped at me. "Flo," she said. "Has Grandma managed to brainwash you? Has all her ghoul talk finally made you crack? Have you become a ghoul believer? Do you really think there are ghouls – big, dribbly, EXTINCT ghouls – somewhere inside this mountain? Digging their way out?"

I looked at the floor. Put like that it sounded stupid. "I don't know," I mumbled. "Maybe. It's just… I wonder if, well…"

Then I took a deep breath, because I was nervous about what I was going to say. But I still said it.

"Hetty, would *Dad* be so quick to believe Grandma was wrong about ghouls?" I said. "Would he?"

Hetty started to shake her head with a fierce look on her face. "Flo, no," she said. "I told you. Do

NOT talk to me about Dad. Not, not, *not*."

"But, Hetty," I said. "I *need* to. Because Dad always told us to listen to Grandma. So I just wondered...What would Dad think? What would Dad do? If he was here?"

"Dad is NOT here," Hetty hissed. Then she pointed at the door. "Now, go," she said. Then she glared.

So I went to see Mum, who was packing for Conference.

"Mum," I said, perching on the edge of her bed. "Is there any chance, do you think. . . Any chance at all that Grandma could be ... well, *right* about ghouls?"

Mum started to look angry, and I thought she was angry with me – but she wasn't. "Has Grandma been telling you MORE ghoul nonsense?" she hissed. "Filling your head with ridiculous scare stories?"

"Well, I don't know if it's more ghoul nonsense or ridiculous scare stories," I said. "That's the problem. She *did* tell me about the ghouls, and their knobbly fists, and how they'll prowl about sniffing out witchchildren to grab and—"

"Witchchildren to *grab*?" hissed Mum.

"Yes," I said. "Wriggling, squirming, *screaming* witchchildren. And I just wondered if you were sure—"

"Wriggling, squirming, *screaming* witchchildren?" shrieked Mum. And once again she had smoke coming out of her ears.

"Enough," she snapped. "ENOUGH!"

Then she marched over to her desk, opened a drawer and got something out. A big floppy book thing.

"Flo," she said. "Follow me!"

Grandma was in the sitting room. Still staring into the magic mirror.

"Here are the rules this weekend, Mother," said Mum, marching through the doorway and across the room.

"One. You will NOT scare my daughter. She has had *enough* scares in her life for one witchchild. Two. You will NOT mention ghouls. Three. You will choose a room."

Then she slapped the book thing down on Grandma's lap. "Here," she said. "This is the brochure for Heckles Haghome. Choose a room. Nothing cheap, nothing below price bracket four – I will NOT have *Scoop!* saying I am a CRUEL witchdaughter. You can have the best room, the best help witchmedics can give. But after this weekend you are OUT."

I have never seen Mum so angry. She glared right in Grandma's face, swivelled round, started marching back towards the door – and there was a snapping sound.

I looked down. There on the floor, under Mum's foot, was Grandma's wand. Grandma's best wand. Snapped in two.

"Kristabel," hissed Grandma. "That was very clumsy. And now – *now* – I have only one wand left. And that wand, that nasty little wand, Kristabel, is OUR ONLY HOPE of saving witches from a ghoul attack!"

But Mum just swirled out of the room.

✳

Two hours later, Mum was ready to go. Standing in the hallway, with me and Hetty. Then Grandma came out of the sitting room.

"Kristabel," Grandma said, her mouth pinched tight. "I will ask you one more time. Forget about Conference. Cancel it. We MUST keep watch. Plan. Warn witches to prepare for a ghoul attack."

"Cancel *Conference*?" hissed Mum.

Then Grandma turned to Hetty. "As for your

166

Prom, Hetty – cancel that too. Do NOT go," she said. "Skritchetts must stick together, in case of ghoul attack."

"Not *go*?" said Hetty, gaping at Grandma. "NOT GO TO MY PROM?" Then she marched off to her room, packed a bag and came back.

"I am staying at Gigi's tonight," she snapped. Then headed straight out.

As for Mum…

"I shall be out of contact," she said, glaring at Grandma. "I shall not answer my skychatter or return calls – unless it is a TOTAL emergency."

"Ghouls *will* be a total emergency, Kristabel," said Grandma. "The first ghoul attack will be only the beginning. There will be more. Then more still. Until ALL witchchildren, ALL witches in Haggspit will be ghouls."

There was a toot from outside. Mum's skycab.

Mum picked up her bags. Marched to the front door.

"Kristabel," said Grandma. "Stay. Skritchetts MUST work together, work as a team. Skritchetts are the only witches who know. Skritchetts must deal with the ghoul attack."

Mum turned. Angry flames were flickering out of her eyes. "Skritchetts will *not* work together," she hissed. "Skritchetts are *not* a team. And Skritchetts will *not* deal with a ghoul attack. Because ghouls are EXTINCT!"

Then she slammed out of the front door. I heard the roar of the skycab engine, and Mum was gone.

Part
Three

Chapter 26

The house was strange. Silent. No Mum, no Hetty. Just me and Grandma. But not the Grandma I knew. No cackling. No jokes. No banging about in the kitchen, chucking things in cauldrons, wailing witchy songs.

No. Grandma just sat and stared. Stared into the magic mirror.

Outside, skyriders flew overhead. Skyshuttles, skyshredders, all kinds of skyriders. All full of witchkids. Witchkids worrying about normal things – like forgetting their gripball kit, or not having done their witchcitizenship homework.

NOT worrying about ghouls…

Ghouls.

I huddled down next to Grandma.

Because the wondering, the doubts – they were gone. I had no doubts left. None.

The pelloligans migrating… The knocking noises… The autumn trees… Grandma was right. They were all signs. They *were*.

"Grandma," I said. "It *is* true, isn't it? Ghouls really ARE on their way."

"Flo," said Grandma grimly. "They are."

"Grandma," I said. "If there are ghouls, if ghouls do come – what about a magiquake? Can we create a magiquake?"

But straight away I knew the answer.

No.

No witch can control elementals. Not ordinary elementals, like storms and blizzards. And definitely not magic elementals, like magiquakes. It was impossible. Some things are too big, even for magic to do.

Which left only one thing.

Grandma's plan.

"Grandma," I said. "Your plan – taking doppel potion, luring ghouls to an ambush, finding a spell to get rid of them, and the thousands of witches to

172

do it… Is it going to *work*?"

"Flo," said Grandma. "It HAS to."

"But, Grandma," I said. "Suppose something goes wrong? Suppose the potion isn't strong enough? Suppose it doesn't fool them? Then you'll be in the middle of a ghoul swarm, defenceless. And suppose you never turn back? Or suppose the wand—"

"Suppose you stop asking questions," Grandma snapped.

But I couldn't. So *much* could go wrong with Grandma's plan.

"Grandma," I said. "Are you sure ghouls *can* be lured? Suppose ghouls are too stupid to understand your luring? Suppose ghouls don't *want* to be lured? And—"

But Grandma's lips made a thin tight line. "Do you have a BETTER plan?" she barked.

"No," I said.

"Well then," Grandma said.

Then she leaned forward. Stared right into the magic mirror. At the autumn leaves. As one, two – a few more – began to flutter off the trees. Drop to the ground.

"Winter is beginning," said Grandma. "Ghouls are near."

"How near?" I said, moving closer to her. "Grandma, *how* near? How long until the ghoul attack?"

"I don't know, Flo," Grandma said. "Maybe a week. Maybe days. I just don't know."

But Grandma was wrong.

It wasn't a week. It wasn't even days.

The ghoul attack was only *hours* away…

★

That night there were storms in Haggspit. The shadows grew long, the sky went dark and the storm swept in from the sea.

Thunder crashed. Lightning flashed. And still Grandma sat. Sat and stared.

I got a blanket. Pulled it right round me, huddled on the sofa. I didn't want to be in my room. It was too far away. Too alone.

And Mum… Hetty… I wanted them here. *Now.*

They'll be back, I told myself. It's not long – just two days. Two days, then we'll convince them. Make them believe about ghouls. We *will.*

The clock struck midnight. Struck one. Struck two. Struck three. And I thought I'd NEVER sleep – but I did.

I slept, and I dreamed. More muddled, terrifying dreams.

Dreams of thunder and lightning, of blizzards and fire.

Dreams of Grandma, of Mum, and of Hetty – all screaming, all running from ghouls.

Dreams of Dad and the Claws, coming out of the ground behind him.

And dreams of my Shudders. Those glimpses, those scenes, those strange twisted shapes in the sky.

And all through the night that noise, that loud evil snarling – it haunted each one of my dreams.

Then I woke, and the storm was gone.

I sat up, rubbed my eyes, checked my watch. Almost seven o'clock. A new day. Saturday. Fresh and quiet and peaceful. The suns glinting way above. Witchenwater sparkling far below.

And beside me Grandma, staring into her magic mirror.

Then Grandma sat forward. Took a sharp – *sharp* – breath. Stared closer.

So I stared too…

At a thin white frost spreading across the ground. Spreading up the trees. Spreading over the leaves.

At the leaves – gold leaves, red leaves, yellow and copper and orange leaves, all shapes, all sizes, all kinds of leaves – all curling up. All shrivelling. All beginning to drop.

Dropping slowly at first, then faster and faster. Tumbling off the trees. Heaping up in big piles. Lying withered and crinkled, then still.

Until the trees stood alone. Just bare winter branches, drooping and grey.

Then the trees started to tremble, to shake...

The leaves, in their heaps, started to rustle, to quiver...

As if the ground *itself* was moving.

A trail of green smoke curled upwards. Green smoky breath...

Then I saw it.

A shape.

A shape – monstrous and grinning and green. Heaving itself out of the ground. A spiny back and spiny wings. Huge arms, huge legs and a cruel, curved mouth.

And behind it, more shapes. More and more and more...

Ghouls. They were here.

Chapter 27

GRATED DRAGON'S TOOTH

DRIED TROLL TOENAILS

Ghouls ... standing tall and strong and scaly, flapping huge spiny wings.

Ghouls ... soaring into the air, and swooping off down Moaning Mountain.

Grandma leapt to her feet. "No time to waste, Flo," she said. "Within minutes those ghastly creatures will attack!"

Then she hitched up her robes and sprinted to the kitchen. Grabbed the doppel potion and headed straight for the back door.

I sprinted after her. "Grandma," I said, clutching her hand. "Are you *sure* you should do this?"

"Flo," said Grandma. "I am."

Then she shooed me away.

"Stay inside, Flo," she said. "A tiny part of my brain will, I imagine, still be me – but a much *much* larger part will be ghoul."

"But, Grandma—" I said.

"INSIDE!" Grandma barked.

I pressed my hands against the kitchen window, and watched.

Watched Grandma – a small black figure in a big green garden – whip the wand out of her robe pocket. Watched her wag her finger at it as it jiggled. Watched her shout at it to behave itself.

Watched her tap it against the potion bottle – *hard*.

Once.

Twice.

Three times.

The potion started to bubble and pop. Trails of green smoke flickered out through the glass.

The wand jiggled and jiggled, struggling to get free.

And it did.

It flew out of Grandma's hand. Hurled itself skywards – up and up and up. Then a shower of stardust shot out of the end...

It took seconds.

Seconds for that small stubby wand to turn into something else.

Something huge and feathery and purple. With a big, curving beak and round, goggling eyes. With scraggly green wings and pink gangly legs. Like a gigantic bird – tall as a witchman – drawn by a four-year-old witchkid.

I gaped. What was happening? What was the wand doing? Was it backsurging? Was that what this was? If so it was very strange backsurging indeed. Not a spell on Grandma, but a spell on itself.

But … why?

Was the wand confused? Upset by Grandma's shouting? Cross at being held so tight?

Whatever the reason, the wand – the something – was NOT happy. Not happy being whatever it was. And not happy with Grandma. Not happy *at all*.

Because the something gave a loud squawk. A furious squawk. It flapped its huge scraggly wings. It circled over Grandma. Then it dived.

Grandma tried to dodge.

She failed.

With one swipe of the furious squawking something's big beak, Grandma went flying, hurtling across the garden.

Then she landed. Splayed out in a flowerbed, both eyes shut tight. Knocked out cold.

I ran outside. Crouched down. "Grandma, open your eyes," I said.

But Grandma didn't.

And beside her, the strange squawking something started shrinking, changing – turning back into what it once was.

A small stubby wand, lying jiggling in the grass. Jiggling sheepishly. Jiggling guiltily…

Then Grandma started snoring. Long, loud snores. The snores of a deep, shocked sleep. So I half carried, half dragged her into the house. Laid her down on the sofa, covered her with a blanket.

Then, just for a moment, Grandma *did* open her eyes. Woozy, astonished eyes. She sat up, grabbed my arm. "Flo," she said. "Ghouls. Ghouls!"

But that was it. She flopped back down. And her eyes once more shut tight.

So I panicked.

Would Grandma be all right? She *looked* all right – a healthy green glow to her cheeks. She was just snoring a lot. But how long would she stay like that, snoring and shocked? And what about me? What should *I* do now? Sit here and wait for her to wake up?

And I panicked more. Because I knew the answer.

No. I *couldn't* wait.

The ghoul attack had begun – and only two witches knew. Two witches in the whole of Haggspit, in the whole of Witchworld.

Grandma.

And me.

Chapter 28

Now, I like reading about witchgirls doing brave things. I like watching witchgirls do brave things on screen – like Destiny Daggett in *Skyhunter* – but that doesn't mean I want to do them myself.

Like I said, I'm scared of lots of things. And since the Claws I'm even more scared of even more things.

I knew that right now I *should* do something brave. That Destiny Daggett would do that, in my position.

But Destiny was invented by grown-up witches. Witches whose job was to invent tricky situations to stick Destiny in. Then make it look impossible for Destiny to get out of the tricky situations. And, finally, come up with a sneaky way for Destiny to manage it.

But I *wasn't* invented. And I had no grown-up to come up with a sneaky way to get me out of my tricky situation. I didn't have anyone. Only me. Florence Skritchett – extremely ordinary witchkid.

And I did NOT want to take Grandma's doppel potion. Grandma's untried, untested doppel potion.

So I called Mum.

Mum didn't answer.

I left her a message. A panicking message, telling her about Grandma, about the ghouls. A rambling, jabbering, all-over-the-place sort of message – but the best I could do.

Surely Mum would check her messages. Even at Conference. They'd have a break sometime. She'd check her skychatter then. She *would*.

Then I switched on the witchscreen. Breaking news was just coming in.

Witchbabies – lots of them – were missing from Hallows Home Orphanage.

Oh no. Oh no no no.

Hallows Home Orphanage – near the foot of Moaning Mountain. We passed it on the way to Harridan's. I saw them out in the garden, a little row of buggies. Little fat legs, little fat arms waving in the sun.

Little orphan witchbabies… Big hungry ghouls…

Those poor, *poor* witchbabies.

And Grandma's words echoed round and round in my head…

"*The first ghoul attack will be only the beginning. There will be more. Then more still. Until ALL witchchildren, ALL witches in Haggspit will be ghouls.*"

So I called the emergency services. Said it was ghouls that took the witchbabies and that there'd be another attack around seven this evening.

Straight away the witch on the other end started hissing. "If this is your idea of a joke," she hissed, "it is a vicious and spiteful one." Then she cut me off.

I panicked. What now? What should I do? Who else could I call? The government? Vermin control?

Who would listen? Who would believe me? Who would take charge, deal with the ghouls? Someone had to.

Then I panicked more, because I knew the answer…

No one.

I wanted to howl, I really did. I wanted to sit at

the kitchen table, put my head in my hands and howl.

Because Grandma said Skritchetts must save Witchworld – but I didn't see how Skritchetts possibly could. Because I knew what I had to do – but I did NOT want to.

But I didn't howl. Instead, I thought about Dad, what he said to me.

"*It's the witchgirls who do things when they're scared. They're the truly brave ones.*"

Well, today I *was* scared. More scared than I had ever been. But today, I HAD to be brave.

And I would be.

I just had one more to call to make.

And Hetty *did* answer.

"Henrietta Skritchett," she said happily. "On the morning of her Prom. Having just found the perfect purple lipstick to complete her Prom outfit. Speak, annoying brat."

"Hetty," I said. "*Hetty!* There really *are* ghouls. I saw them."

Hetty gave a cackle of laughter. "Weirdo," she screeched.

"Hetty," I said. "Listen. There's lots of them, and they're BIG and I've got to take doppel potion and find out how to get rid of them, and lure them to an ambush, and I wanted to speak to you first, say goodbye, just in case anything goes wrong, and—"

But all of a sudden Hetty was gone, the skychatter snatched off her. And then I heard Gigi's voice.

"This is Henrietta Skritchett's personal answering service," Gigi said, putting on a pretending-to-be-a-message voice. "She is unable to take calls from teenies because she is busy busy busy preparing for her Prom."

Then Gigi cut me off.

So I went out in the garden. I opened the small green bottle of doppel potion. I poured three sparkling drops into the tiny silver spoon with shaking hands…

One.

Two.

Three.

And I drank…

Just as my skychatter pinged – and a message came through from Hetty.

YOU NEVER LIE. ON WAY BACK. X

Chapter 29

GRATED DRAGON'S TOOTH

DRIED TROLL TOENAILS

It started with goose bumps. Goose bumps that popped up all over my arms, my legs. My teeth began to clack. I went cold – cold as a slab of serpent steak, packed in ice at the fish shop.

My skin grew darker, scalier, slimier.

Every bone in my body squirmed. Squirmed, and felt strange. Like I was bones, but elastic, all at once.

I panicked. I wanted it to stop. *Now.*

But it didn't.

My shoes vanished. Two bony green feet took their place.

My hands grew. Changed from small witchkid

hands into big ghoul hands. Strong hands. Knobbly hands. Hands with six stubby fingers.

Hands for grabbing, for holding, for crushing. Hands that scared me.

I started to stretch. I stretched in big jerking bursts. One burst, then another, and another.

I staggered. I must be seven foot tall now, towering on big ghoul legs. I felt dizzy, like being up a ladder – but with no way to hold on.

Now something was straining and struggling, trying to burst out from inside my shoulders, my huge ghoul shoulders...

Something did.

Wings the size of sails. Spiny wings, vast and powerful. Wings in four strong sections.

And my ears, my eyes ... they were different.

I could hear things a witchkid can't. The ground breathing. Insect feet pattering. Mermaids humming.

And I could see the tiniest things, far far away. Ants at the foot of Moaning Mountain. Corals at the bottom of Witchenwater.

Then I sniffed. I could smell something...

The ghoul swarm.

Something surged inside me. The swarm. *My* swarm...

188

Witchworld

I wanted to seek them out. To be with them.

Now thoughts were creeping through my brain. Cruel thoughts, vicious thoughts. Thoughts of hunting, of tracking, of attacking. Thoughts of biting.

Thoughts of witchkids.

Then I saw one.

Hetty.

Coming out of the back door, calling my name.

She took one look at me – the ghoul-me, licking my lips as I stared at her with hungry ghoul eyes – and she shrieked.

"No way!" she shrieked. "I absolutely do NOT want to be a ghoul. I haven't even had a BOYFRIEND!" Then she ran.

So I flapped my huge ghoul wings, took off, and soared after her.

✦

Yes, I'm sorry to admit that, but it's what happened.

Because a tiny part of my brain was still me, Flo – a tiny tiny part. That part was saying, "Stop! STOP!"

But a bigger part of me – a much much bigger part of me – was ghoul. And the ghoul-part of me was saying, "Feed! FEED!"

That was the part that made me soar in through the kitchen door and leap – in three huge bounding leaps – across the kitchen and over the worktop. The part that made me pin Hetty to the kitchen wall.

And Hetty was shrieking. Shrieking and shrieking and shrieking. Punching and jabbing and doing her best to fight the ghoul-me off – as I towered above her, growling and hissing.

✶

Even now I don't know what would have happened. Whether I really would, or *could*, have turned my own sister into a ghoul – but just then three nibbet heads poked out of a hole in the wall.

Up to that point, this is what I knew about nibbets:

Nibbets are bad-tempered.
Nibbets live in most witch houses, including mine.
Nibbets are tiny and blue, with long rattling
    tails.
Nibbets have pointy teeth, sharp as daggers.
Nibbets gnaw stuff in cupboards – any stuff –
    with those pointy teeth.
Nibbets leave little blue droppings wherever
    they go.
Nibbets make scrabbling noises in walls at
    night.
If you block up a nibbet hole, a nibbet makes
    two new ones.

Nibbets are a nuisance.

But now I learned something new about nibbets:

Nibbets are not always a nuisance...
Because ghouls are terrified of nibbets.

As soon as I saw those three tiny heads, those three tiny sets of bristling whiskers, those three tiny sets of gnashing teeth, I felt my big ghoul legs start to shake. I let out a big ghoul howl, then a whimper. And I started blundering and swirling round the kitchen. Terrified.

And as I blundered I started to feel strange. To change. To grow bits of other things – the stubby green arm of a dragon, the hairy feet of a troll, the swishing tail of a mermaid, the curving horn of a unicorn. And then to shrink, in big jerking bursts... Until, in the end, it was over. I was me again. Slumped in the middle of the kitchen floor.

Knowing one thing for sure. That Grandma's doppel potion needed more work.

But that wasn't the only thing I knew. Oh no.

Being a ghoul, attacking Hetty, I knew something else too. Something MUCH more important.

Chapter 30

I think it was the shrieking that did it. Hetty shrieking and shrieking as she fought against the ghoul-me.

Piercing witchteen shrieks…

Like a *dinner bell* to a ghoul, that's what Grandma said.

And that's when I realised. That's when I knew. A place we could lure the ghouls to. The *perfect* place for a ghoul attack, for an ambush.

A place packed with witchteens, a place full of lights, full of noise… Hetty's Prom.

Hetty was clutching on to the worktop. Staring down at me and pointing. Struggling to speak.

"Y-y-you—" she said. "You ... then ... just now ... That ghoul ... That actual *ghoul* ... The ghoul that attacked me – it was *you*."

It was all too for much for Hetty.

She slithered down the worktop, then slumped next to me on the floor.

"Hetty," I said. "I'm sorry I attacked you. It's just... Grandma's doppel potion didn't work quite right – as you saw. But that doesn't *matter*, Hetty, because now I know something. Something really important. I know what we have to do. A way we might stop the ghoul attack... And first, we have to make the ghouls attack your Prom!"

Hetty's mouth dropped open. She sat, gaping at me. Totally silent. Still slumped.

"Ghouls are attracted by noise," I said. "*Noise*, Hetty! Noise, like the gurgles of witchbabies, and the happy shouts of witchkids. But the piercing shrieks of witchteens, Hetty – they're like a DINNER BELL to a ghoul!"

Hetty gaped more.

"And, Hetty, ghouls like *light*. Bright lights – and your Prom will have lots of lights. Flashing lights. Fireworks. And the buildings, the gardens – they'll all be lit up. And there'll be noise, lots of noise. And there'll be music, loud music. And witchteens, lots of them. And those witchteens – you and your friends, Hetty – have to *lure* the ghouls by shrieking, by screaming. And the more noise you make, the more likely the ghouls are to be lured!"

The words were tumbling out of my mouth now. And I knew I was right. That this was a plan. A chance. Our *only* chance.

"And the timing, Hetty – it's perfect!" I said. "Because hungry ghouls – and Grandma says most of them are – attack *twice* a day. Once every twelve hours. Which means the next ghoul attack will be soon after seven o'clock this evening. SEVEN, Hetty. The time your Prom starts!"

My mind was racing, my mouth struggling to keep up. "So, we *lure* the ghouls to your Prom, Hetty – then I lock them in. There's a spell I know that will keep you safe, so I'll do that. And Mum can meet us there with thousands and *thousands* of witches. And they have to do a spell too. Only their spell will be one to get rid of the ghouls – and they will. They WILL!"

And still Hetty sat gaping – but I couldn't stop talking. Because Dad's words were going round and round in my head.

194

"*Some futures, Flo, you can MAKE happen.*"

And I knew. *This* future – we HAD to make it happen.

"This is our big chance, Hetty," I said. "A chance to *stop* the ghoul attack. To save witches in Haggspit, witches everywhere! And – yes – there are one or two problems with my plan, like I can't get hold of Mum and I don't know what spell she needs to do. But those problems will have to be SOLVED, Hetty. And Grandma – she was right! Skritchetts WILL save Witchworld!"

Then I ran out of breath.

And Hetty sat, gaping at me. Then she stopped gaping. Her eyes lit up, started gleaming – and I don't know what I expected her to say, but not this...

"I knew it!" she said triumphantly. "I was right! The Accident – it DID do something to your brain!"

I slumped.

All that effort, all that big long speech, and Hetty just thought I had Confusions because of the Accident. Because of the skragglehead sending me flying. Because of me landing on my head.

But no. That *wasn't* what Hetty thought. And that wasn't what Hetty meant. Because she grabbed my arm, and then she said this:

"Your Shudders, Flo," she said, eyes gleaming.

"They're NOT like Great-Grandma's. You don't see witchhistory. You see the *future*!"

The moment Hetty said it, I knew she was right.

It all fell into place. My Shudders, those things I saw in Hurlstruk House – those glimpses, those scenes, all those things that flashed past my eyes – that's what they were.

Not the past, not like Great-Grandma's Shudders. But the future.

The ghoul attack on Hetty's Prom.

I had no idea how, no idea why. Maybe Hetty was right. Maybe it *was* the Accident that did something to my brain. Or maybe I could Shudder both ways. See the past and the future. I just didn't know.

But one thing I DID know.

If my Shudders really *did* see the future, really did see the ghouls attack Hetty's Prom, then – somewhere in those Shudders, somewhere in all those things I saw – was the answer. The solution.

The spell to get rid of ghouls.

Chapter 31

I will never understand witchteens. Especially Hetty. Because Hetty was sitting there, *beaming* at the idea of a ghoul attack on her Prom.

"Flo," she said, eyes shining. "This fate is absolutely the most *thrilling* fate that has EVER happened to me! This fate is like being in a real-life witchscreen adventure. Starring mainly me. ME!"

Then she clasped her hands together. "And when it's all over, and the story of the Skritchetts and the ghoul attack is turned into a major witchscreen movie – I can star as myself. As ME! And be famous!"

Because Hetty – when she's not dreaming of

a boyfriend or a nose job – is dreaming of being famous.

Now Hetty was nodding. "Luring! Luring the ghouls. I'll be an excellent lurer, Flo, I promise! I'll LEAD the luring."

Then Hetty let out a shriek – so loud, so piercing, I clapped my hands to my ears.

"Like that," she said proudly. "That's my luring shriek."

"Hetty, shush," I said. "There are *problems*. First problem is I can't get hold of Mum – and she's got to get thousands of witches to your Prom so they can do the spell to get rid of ghouls."

"NOT a problem, Flo," Hetty said, shaking her head. She checked her watch. "It's early. Not even ten. Conference has breaks. Witches making speeches, then breaks. That's what happens ALL day at Conference. Speeches then breaks. Mum'll check for messages in the first break. That's when she'll get the thousands of witches."

Well, I hoped Hetty was right.

"Continue," Hetty said, still beaming. "Your second problem is. . .?"

"There's two spells that have to happen, Hetty," I said. "One spell to keep you safe – which I know. And one spell to get rid of ghouls – which I don't.

Maybe I saw the spell in my Shudders ... but they were so fast, they weren't clear, they didn't make sense."

"Also not a problem," Hetty said, beaming more. "Regress, Flo. That's what you have to do."

"Regress?" I said, baffled.

Hetty nodded. "Do this," she said. Then she screwed her eyes tight shut.

"Pretend you are back at Hurlstruk House," she instructed, eyes still tight shut. "Walk up the steps, in through the doors. Go through everything that happened, everything you saw with your Shudders. Go slow – SLOOOOW, Flo. And in the end your Shudders will be *totally* clear, and you'll find the answer!"

She opened her eyes again. "That's regressing," she said. "Simple!"

Well, it didn't sound simple to me.

Then Hetty stood up. "You're brainy, Flo," she said, beaming again. "You'll be an excellent regresser. And while you are regressing – I have nails to attend to. If I'm going to be ghoul bait I'm going to look *good*!"

Then she clacked off out of the kitchen.

I tried to regress. I sat there with my eyes tight shut

and I tried and tried – but I could NOT make myself regress. Because each time I shut my eyes, a horrible thought popped into my head.

Suppose the regressing *did* work, did make my Shudders much clearer… But suppose my Shudders showed me something I did *not* want to see?

Like a grisly future. A gory, horrifying future. A future where we DIDN'T stop the ghoul attack. A future where all those screaming, struggling witchteens – including Hetty – were turned into ghouls themselves…

So I sat quaking and quaking, not at all sure that regressing was something I wanted to do.

And muddled, panicking thoughts swirled around in my brain. Thoughts about Mum not getting in touch. Thoughts about how fast time was passing. Thoughts about Grandma, all the things she said about ghouls. And thoughts – again and again, but I didn't know why – of just one bit of my Shudders, just one.

Those twisted shapes in the sky…

Why did I keep thinking about them? *Why?* I had no idea.

But slowly, slowly, something was happening. Something was connecting. Something Grandma said about ghouls. And those twisted shapes in the sky, what they might be…

And I had a feeling, growing stronger, that the answer was just out of reach. Like two pieces of a jigsaw that just needed fitting together.

Then, in the end – like a *ting* in my head – it all made sense.

And I knew. There *was* a spell. A spell Mum and her witches could do. A spell that might STOP the ghoul attack.

✳

So I called Mum, then I mailed Mum. Left long rambling messages explaining everything.

Then I ran into Hetty's room. "Hetty! I worked out the spell to get rid of ghouls," I said. "But Mum's STILL not answering. I just got the out-of-office message. What do we do? What do we *do*?"

"Flo," said Hetty, sitting on her bed, tutting and waving her fingers about to dry her nails. "You keep seeing problems where are there ARE none. It's almost eleven. First break will be any moment."

"But … is that long enough?" I said. "Enough time for Mum to organise everything?"

"It is," said Hetty confidently. "Mum's *job* is organising things. She can organise this. Easy."

Then she pointed her nails at me. "Admire," she said, beaming. "I gave them an extra coat, so they should survive the ghoul attack without chipping. But, Flo, you *must* do that spell to keep us safe as SOON as the last ghoul is inside the Prom—"

Hetty stopped. Stopped talking. Stopped beaming. Went pale. "Oh…" she said.

And that was when I realised. I thought there were only two problems with my plan. But I was wrong.

There were *three*.

Chapter 32

GRATED DRAGON'S TOOTH

DRIED TROLL TOENAILS

I don't know what spell laws you witchkids in other landzones have – but here in United Witchenlands, us witchkids have a LOT of spell laws. Way too many.

And although I knew a spell to keep Hetty safe, I had forgotten one small detail.

I had no way of doing it.

Hetty started wailing now. "My big chance to be famous! Snatched away from me! Gone!" she wailed. "Spellsticks – no use! Wands – no use! We're all *doomed*!"

And Hetty was right. I started to panic. How

could I do the spell? *How?*

Not using my under-twelve spellstick — that would explode if I used it outside the classroom. And Hetty's under-sixteen spellstick — that *would* work, but only for under-sixteen spells, which this spell was NOT.

And grown-up spellsticks had too much security for me to use, and wands had WIN numbers — Witch Identification Numbers. All old wands have to have WIN numbers, so only the wand's owner can use it. It's been the law for seven years…

Which was when I got a glimmer of an idea.

"Hetty," I said.

"Not now, Flo," wailed Hetty. "I am *grieving*! Grieving for us witchteens — denied the chance to be famous! Cut down in our prime! Turned into ghoul dinner! Grieving for Skritchetts! Grieving for Witchworld! Soon we'll all be GHOULS!"

In the end I had to shake her. "Hetty," I said. "STOP wailing. I'm trying to tell you something. Wands — they have WIN numbers."

"I know, Flo, I know!" Hetty wailed. "It's the law!"

"*That's* what I'm trying to tell you," I said. "The LAW, Hetty! A big important law! The law of South Witchenland!"

Hetty's mouth snapped shut. She stopped wailing. Then her eyes started gleaming. At last – she'd got it.

Then we both leapt up. We both charged out into the back garden.

"There!" pointed Hetty. "There!"

And I grabbed it. The small stubby wand, jiggling in the grass.

Because – like I said – Grandma doesn't take too much notice of laws.

✦

Grandma's *Beginner Wand Skills and Spells Book* was a huge, heavy thing. Her old school textbook – five hundred and seventy pages long, and all splatted with ink blots and smears.

On page one it said this:

BEWARE BACKSURGE!

Witchchildren. You MUST use the CORRECT magic words, in the CORRECT order, with the CORRECT pronunciation, and the CORRECT pauses.

You must also make sure your wand-waving is ACCURATE, so study all diagrams with CARE.

If you STUMBLE over your magic words, or do

SLOPPY wand-waving, your wand may BACKSURGE. It will do your spell - but then do a spell on YOU.*

Any witchchild who sees a classmate fall victim to backsurge should alert their witchteacher IMMEDIATELY.

I gulped. Then I read the footnote.

*Note: Wands are living things. Just as plants may not all flourish and grow in the same way, not all wands may work as well as they should.

If your wand has three backsurge incidents in a row, your teacher must check the wand for defects. You may have a FAULTY wand.

Oh no. I thought about Grandma. What she said.

   "*Jiggles about. Fidgets. Nasty little thing. Faulty, in my opinion.*"

   And I thought of the wand.

   How it shot out of Grandma's hand. How it backsurged in that strange and peculiar way. How Grandma was still lying there, knocked out by her very own wand. *This* wand. The wand I was going to use...

I gulped more.

Then I had a talk to the wand.

"I don't think you're faulty," I said to the wand. "I DO think you jiggle and fidget, but that doesn't mean you're faulty."

I was in the sitting room, on the sofa. The wand – still jiggling – was lying on my lap.

"I think you're unhappy," I said. "I think Grandma makes you nervous when she shouts at you for jiggling. And she grips you too tight when you jiggle, and it hurts – so you jiggle even more."

It sounds strange, but it felt like the wand was listening. It was hardly jiggling at all now.

"It can't be nice being a wand for a witch who shouts. Who thinks you're a menace," I said. "And I think that's why you backsurged. Not because you're faulty. But because you're unhappy and nervous and hurting. Confused. I don't think you *meant* to backsurge. I think you just couldn't help doing it."

Then I gave the wand a stroke. It felt warm. Like a living thing. Like it was … well – *breathing*.

"A wand that jiggles and fidgets can still be a very good wand," I said. "And I need your help. I have to do a big spell – but I'm only a learner. I've never used a wand before. So if I get things wrong, I'm sorry. But I'll do my best, really I will."

I stroked it again. "You and me, we can be a good team," I said. "And if we do the spell right, you will be the most important wand in Haggspit. Maybe even in Witchworld."

Then – or was I imagining it? I wasn't sure – I thought I heard the tiniest sound. Almost as if the wand was purring.

The spell, when we finally found it, was on page 342. And it took almost *all day* to learn it, to learn how to do it. Because using a wand is hard – nothing like using a spellstick. No in-built spell package, no spellsearch, no spellsplice. Nothing quick. Nothing easy.

Just lots and lots of magic words, and lots and lots of wand-waving.

And this spell was seventeen words long. *Seventeen*. It also had twenty-three separate wand-waving movements.

The first words I had to say in the spell were these: "*Abrakkida Mutattik*." Which look quite simple written like that.

They weren't.

Because there was a guide showing how to pronounce it. This:

Witchworld

Ab/ậïïrrr- — ậ – kk/eee/ -dùh /// Mùuuu – tậ – tï -/kk

Those squiggles, those dashes, all those lines you can see – every single one of them meant something different.

As for the wand-waving, there were swooping motions, looping motions, jabbing motions and pauses. And every wand-wave had its own diagram.

"Flo," said Hetty nervously, looking over my shoulder. "It is a VERY good thing you are brainy."

So I practised.

I practised and practised and practised. I practised until my head was spinning and my arms were aching.

I practised the words, then I practised the wand-waving – using a knife from the cutlery drawer to stand in as a wand. Then I practised them both together.

All day long I got Hetty to test me. Again and again, and again.

Until at last I got it right.

But there was STILL no word from Mum.

Chapter 33

Mum. Where WAS she? Why didn't she answer? My calls, my webmail, they'd all reached her, I knew they had.

Because my skychatter supplier – like Hetty's, like most witchkids in South Witchenland – is Babblechat. And Babblechat lets you know if your calls or webmail don't get through. Babblechat beeps and flashes up one of two signs.

Which it did now.

Because I tried – *again* – to call Mum, to webmail her. But both times, Babblechat beeped. Then it flashed up the signs:

Witchworld

CALL DID NOT CONNECT
WEBMAIL DID NOT DELIVER

Oh no. No, no, NO. Now I couldn't get through to Mum at all.

But *why* hadn't Mum called me earlier? My earlier calls, my webmails, they'd all got through.

Was she too busy with Conference to check for calls and webmail?

No. Even at Conference Mum would check in case I was trying to get in touch. She would.

Or maybe she *did* check her calls and webmail – and now she was too busy to call me? Too busy organising, getting those thousands of witches to the Prom?

No. Mum would call me no matter how busy she was getting witches. She *would*.

But time ticked by. Three … four … five o'clock … and still no word from her.

I went to see Grandma. Sat and watched as she lay there, snoring and still.

"Grandma," I said. "Please wake up. You HAVE to wake up. I can't get hold of Mum and I don't know what to do. Please, please wake up."

But Grandma just lay there. Did I see a flicker of one eye almost opening? No. I imagined it.

So I wrote Grandma a note. A long, long note.

"Grandma," I said, tucking it in her hand. "I'm leaving you this note. It tells you what me and Hetty are planning, in case you wake up. But, Grandma – what it doesn't tell you is this. That I am more scared than I have EVER been."

Which I was.

Because I did *not* want the ghouls to attack Hetty's Prom. Not without knowing that Mum and her witches would get there.

But we had to do this. Had to lure the ghouls to the Prom. Because if we didn't – the ghouls would attack somewhere else. Would swarm and attack and feed. Would double, then split – and then there'd be no way to stop them.

Then the ghoul attack would go on. On and on and on. Until every witch in Haggspit – in Witchworld – would end up as ghouls.

Including us.

So we had no choice. We HAD to do this.

Which is what Hetty said. Sort of…

Hetty came clacking into the sitting room, all dressed for her Prom. With her hair piled high, and thick, heavy make-up -- and a pale, pale face underneath.

She sat down beside me, eyes huge and anxious. "Flo," she said, gulping. "About fate… I've been thinking. It is possible that an extremely *bad* fate is ahead for us witchteens. That we lure the ghouls to the Prom but Mum and her witches don't turn up. And with that fate, it is quite likely that some — or most — of us witchteens will become ghouls once your safety spell wears off."

She gave another gulp. "Yes. Mum not turning up, that is a BAD fate, Flo."

Hetty leaned forward, paler than ever. "But, Flo," she said. "There is *another* bad fate. Because you and Mum may save Witchworld -- but Mum may turn up a bit too late for us witchteens."

Now Hetty was knotting her fingers together. "And, Flo, if *that* bad fate happens…" she said. "If the spell wears off and I do, like, get gassed by ghoul breath, and the fatal biters and all that — promise me two things. One, burn my diary. Do NOT look in it and totally do NOT let Mum look in it. And two, if Mum runs an article about the brave and noble witchteens who sacrificed their lives for others — no profile pictures of me. Not with my nose. Straight on, front view only."

I couldn't help it. I gaped. But Hetty hadn't finished.

"Those are the bad fates, Flo," she said, voice wobbling. "But the *good* fate, Flo – that is probably what will happen. That us witchteens do the luring, your spell keeps us safe, and Mum turns up with her witches and gets rid of the ghouls."

She started nodding hard now. "Yes, the good fate, that is almost definitely what will happen," she said. "In fact, Mum will be on her way already, with all those witches. And there'll be a reason she hasn't called. An explanation. Something…"

She tailed off, and I knew why. Because Hetty could NOT think of an explanation, any more than I could.

"Hetty—" I said. Then I stopped. Listened.

I could hear something. Outside, getting louder. The throb of a powerful engine. The engine of a skyswaggerer.

The Harridan's skyswaggerer.

And there it was. Swooping down off Skyway 121. A long, long skyrider – long as a skybus, streaming with banners and balloons. Packed with witchteens, collected up, house by house. And now Hetty…

The final stop before Harridan's.

"Flo," said Hetty, clutching my arm so hard it hurt. "Maybe there's another fate. Maybe we won't need to do this AT ALL. Maybe the government have seen the ghouls on spycam. Have secret ghoul-defence plans. Ghoul poison, or ghoul traps, or…"

Hetty gave up. "Mum," she said, teeth clacking. "Where is she? Where IS she?"

"I don't know," I said, miserable. Utterly miserable. "I don't know if she'll get there at all. Hetty – I'm sorry. It's because of me, my plan, that you're doing this."

"*Someone* has to be ghoul bait, Flo," said Hetty, teeth clacking harder.

"I know," I said, more miserable than ever. "I just wish it wasn't you."

And outside, the skyswaggerer landed.

It was time. Me and Hetty both stood up to go.

"Flo," said Hetty, voice small and wobbling. "I would just like to say that it has been an honour being your sister. And that I am TOTALLY scared. More scared than I have *ever* been."

And I only had one thing to say. "Hetty," I told her. "It's the witchgirls who do things when they're scared – they're the truly brave ones."

Then I hugged Hetty, and Hetty hugged me. And, together, we walked out of the house.

Part
Four

Chapter 34

GRATED DRAGON'S TOOTH

DRIED TROLL TOE-NAILS

It stretched across the front garden. A huge skyswaggerer. The doors slid open and down came a staircase, glittering and gold. The shrieks, the cackles — they were deafening. The shrieks and cackles of excited witchteens. Witchteens with no idea what lay ahead.

"Hetty," I said. "Shouldn't you warn them? Give them the choice?"

"I can't, Flo," said Hetty, shaking her head. "If I warn them, they might not go."

"I know," I said — so SO miserable. "But, well … it just doesn't seem fair."

"It *isn't* fair," said Hetty. "But it's the only way. We have to try this. If we don't, we end up as ghouls anyway."

She put one foot on the first golden step. "It is *showtime*, Flo," she said firmly. "Now I, Henrietta Skritchett, have to do the best, most important lying of my life."

Then she clacked up the big golden stairs – me following behind – and I watched as she switched into action.

"Guys," Hetty said with a big roll of her eyes. "Disaster!" Then she jerked her thumb at me. "Got to babysit the teeny. My dotty old grandma knocked herself out."

The witchteens all groaned.

"I'll stick her in the back after take-off," Hetty said, strapping me and her in a double seat as the skyswaggerer shot upwards. "Shut her in. On her own. Witchteen talk is NOT for witchkid ears."

And when the strap sign went off, Hetty grabbed my arm and marched me off towards the back flexipod. She took one step inside it, then stopped.

"Flo, you're right," she said, shaking her head. "I can't do this. Not this way."

She looked at me, biting her lip. "What is *wrong*

with me?" she said. "Me, the best witchteen liar in Haggspit. And now, just when I really need to – I can't do it. I can't lie. I canNOT send my friends into a ghoul attack. Not like this."

So she marched us both back again. Clapped her hands. "Guys," she said. "I have NEWS!"

✦

Hetty told the witchteens everything.

They sat, mouths open, jaws dropping, eyes popping. There was total silence when she finished. And then…

"So," said Gigi, looking a bit confused. "We're being the ghoul bait. We're doing the luring – shrieking and screaming, making sure the ghouls attack our Prom? And then the teeny will save us? Your teeny?"

They all looked at me doubtfully.

"Wand," said a witchteen, snapping her fingers. "Show me."

So I did.

"It's a very good wand," I told the witchteen. "Me and it, we're a team." Then I stroked it, and it glowed.

"What about your mum?" said another one, narrowing her eyes. "Can she REALLY get all those thousands of her readers together in time?"

"She can," said Hetty. Which wasn't a lie. Because if anyone could do it, Mum could. We just didn't know if she *was*...

Although Hetty left out that bit.

But two witchteens were whispering. Looking at me, then frowning. Looking out at the sky, frowning more. Sitting huddled together, whispering.

Then one of them spoke.

"Hetty," said one of the whisperers. "Ghouls could be quite big. Quite scary..."

"And Hetty," said the other whisperer. "I'm not TOTALLY sure I *want* to be ghoul bait."

Hetty leapt up and stood right at the front of the flexipod. "Guys, I think we should vote," she said, nodding and beaming a big bright smile all round. "Make it fair. Make it official. Do this properly. Because this is a *really* important thing we have the chance to do. So let's make sure you ALL want to be part of it."

Then Hetty began. "So, the vote," she said, looking around at all the witchteens. "Witchteens who do NOT want to be heroes... Witchteens who do NOT want to take part in this RARE opportunity to be the saviours of Haggspit, and also saviours of Witchworld itself..."

She paused. Looked around more.

"Witchteens who do NOT want to become famous, do NOT want to become celebrities and do NOT want to – very possibly – date a member of Kakkle Kru…" she said. "Hands up."

Not one hand went up. Not even the hand of a whisperer.

"And now," Hetty said, nodding and beaming an even bigger, brighter smile. "Witchteens in favour of taking up this thrilling chance, this ONCE-IN-A-LIFETIME opportunity to be ghoul bait. . . Hands up."

Every single hand shot up.

"And, guys," said one of the whisperers, all eager now. "Remember, we have weapons." Then she leapt up, pulled off her shoe and pointed at the spiky heel.

The other whisperer leapt up too. "Never forget the contents of your clutch," she said, whipping out a can of hairspray. "Aim straight for the eyes."

"And," said another witchteen, leaping to join them. "Make *lots* of noise. Shriek like you have never shrieked before. We do NOT want those ghouls going somewhere else. Some other witchteens getting all the glory. We must NOT miss our big chance at stardom."

Like I said, I will NEVER understand witchteens.

Chapter
35

There it was below us. Hurlstruk House. A blaze of
lights. Party lights, flashing on and off. Flashing red
and yellow, orange and purple, blue and green.

The skyswaggerer landed, the doors hissed open,
the staircase went down and the witchteens ran.

Ran down the gold staircase, across the huge
gardens, towards the wide stone steps of Hurlstruk
House.

Ran – shrieking and screaming, loud as they
could.

And then, up in the Harridan's clocktower, a big
booming bell struck out the hour.

DONG! DONG! DONG! DONG! DONG! DONG! DONG!

Seven o'clock.

Fireworks soared up into the big black sky, spelling out a message, then exploding in showers of light and sparks.

WELCOME TO PROM NIGHT!

A NIGHT TO REMEMBER!

Searchlights — long dazzling beams of light — swept across the sky. Flaming torches flared up all over the gardens. Lights twinkled and sparkled in every tree. Music thudded out. Loud, booming music…

Then the huge glass doors of Hurlstruk House slid open.

I scurried through the shadows. Up the steps, on to the terrace of Hurlstruk House.

Then I hid. Behind a tub with a big spiky tree in it — just like the witchteens told me. A place to see, but not be seen.

I crouched down, legs shaking. Watched witchteens, one after another, streaming their way up the huge stone steps, through the glass doors and into the Prom.

Ten, twenty, thirty, more…

Witchteens shrieking. Witchteens screaming. Witchteen voices – loud as they could make them – piercing the big black sky. Carrying far far away.

Like a dinner bell to a ghoul.

Only Hetty, pale and scared, quietly took the key from the door. Slid it across the terrace to me. Then, with one last terrified look back at me, she went in through the doors.

I picked the key up. Zipped it in my robe pocket.

I was ready. Ready to do the spell. Lock the ghouls in. Lock the witchteens in. Hope that Mum and her witches arrived.

I looked up. Scanned the big black sky.

Ghouls…

Somewhere out there, somewhere up in that big black sky – ghouls were on their way. Ghouls, lured by the noise, the lights. Ghouls, wings beating, eyes glinting. Ghouls, with one thought only in each grinning ghoul head. Feed… FEED.

I crouched lower. Terrified.

Hetty, the witchteens – they would all be trapped. Relying on me, on the wand, on the spell. But would the spell even work? How long would it last? How long would it keep them safe? Long enough for Mum and her army to turn up?

But Mum, the witches – *would* they turn up? Where were they? *Where?* There was so much sky – so big, so black – above me. Were they out there, Mum and her army? Were they streaming across the sky even now?

"Mum," I heard myself whimpering. "Where are you? Why haven't you called? Please be on your way. Please, *please* be on your way."

She had to be. HAD to.

But I knew. Just knew. This could all go so HORRIBLY wrong.

Then I saw it. A shimmering, green glow on the horizon.

A swirling mass of green shapes. Green shapes stretched out across the big black sky.

Shapes far away now, above the hills. . .

But shapes getting closer. Closer every second.

The ghoul swarm.

It was here.

Chapter 36

I crouched lower. Tucked myself into a small, tight bundle. Made myself as tiny as I could.

I could hear the beating of giant wings. Feel a wind so cold – so icy cold – it made my teeth start chattering.

Unicorns in the meadow stampeded, then fled. Merboys in the lake dived underwater. Things scuttled through the undergrowth – terrified, panicking things.

And the swirling green shapes swarmed closer. Trees trembling, leaves falling, flowers withering as they flew.

Then they were here.

Swarming past the unicorn meadow... Past the lake... Up the Harridan's gardens...

Towards Hurlstruk House.

Thud thud thud – the ghouls landed.

One then another then another, at the foot of the wide stone steps.

A monstrous swarm of huge shadows.

Ghouls – over two metres tall. Huge legs, huge arms, huge spiny wings. Snarling, hissing shadows. Lit by the light spilling out from Hurlstruk House.

Then – in twos, in threes, in fours – those huge hissing shadows started creeping. Ghoul after ghoul after ghoul...

Creeping, grinning and slobbering. Creeping up the stone steps, looking left, looking right.

Ghouls with sharp teeth, dribbling mouths, vicious eyes, the green smoke of ghoul breath swirling around them.

Creeping closer and closer and closer. So close now I could have reached out and touched one.

Shivers, cold as winter, crept through my body as I crouched.

As I watched those ghouls – those huge hissing shadows – creep right past me...

Then swarm through the open glass door.
And into the Prom.

Screams ripped at my ears. Piercing screams. Panicking screams. Screams of witchteens. Terrified witchteens.

I ran from my hiding place, stood in the doorway.

Ghouls were *everywhere*. Swarming through the room. Ghouls towering and hissing. Ghouls leaping and bounding. Ghouls snarling and spitting. Ghouls flapping huge spiny wings in terrified faces.

And witchteens, witchteachers – they were all screaming, all running, arms flailing, eyes terrified. All panicking, colliding, tripping over each other.

Then – Hetty – I saw Hetty, right at the front of a group of witchteens. Witchteens jabbing and punching and yelling. As ghouls – snarling hissing ghouls – circled around them.

I scrabbled for the wand with icy hands.

The words, get the words right, I told myself. The right words, the right order, the right wand-waving. Keep the witchteens safe. Keep *Hetty* safe.

Then I heard something.

A noise. *That* noise. The loud snarling noise. The menacing, dangerous, EVIL noise. The noise that had haunted my dreams every night since I Shuddered.

A noise that was near. Very near.

And I knew straight away.

Not all the ghouls were in there, in the Prom.

One ghoul was NOT with the swarm. Because one ghoul was hunting alone.

And right behind me.

Chapter 37

I turned – and I quaked. This was no ordinary ghoul.

This was worse. Far worse.

A giant of a ghoul, three times my size. A nightmare of a ghoul. A scaly, stinking, towering monster of a ghoul. With ragged wings and rotting flesh – and a terrible, terrible face.

A brutal face. A savage face. Vicious yellow eyes. A cruel curved beak of a nose. A mouth baring teeth like daggers, all blackened and stinking.

And I knew.

This was the worst ghoul of all. The *rogue* ghoul. The ghoul that hunted alone.

A ghoul so spine-tinglingly, blood-curdlingly terrifying I could NOT move.

It snarled. It hissed. Then it reached out with its hands. It pointed. And…

Click.

Twelve Claws sprang out of its twelve stumpy fingers. Twelve Claws clicked into place. Long, curving Claws. Claws glinting like knives. Claws curving like hooks. Claws as sharp as spears.

Claws for ripping, for tearing, for slashing.

Terrible, terrible Claws.

Claws I'd seen before.

With Dad.

And the memories came flooding back. Of Dad. Of the Claws. Of *everything*.

It was a ghoul. *That* was what I saw. A rogue ghoul, just like this one.

A burst of fireworks lit up the sky. Lit up the ground, all the bushes – and Dad.

Then the Claws – the huge hooked Claws – came out of the ground. And a face, brutal and savage. And strong, strong arms, heaving…

It crawled out of the ground – a cruel cold monster with spikes up its spine and horns on its head. Towered up behind Dad.

I couldn't move. Couldn't speak.

And Dad… Dad was smiling at me. Happy, laughing, ready to light the rocket. As behind him the ghoul reached out with those Claws.

Then Dad's smile was wiped off his face. "Flo," he said. "What is it? What's wrong?"

The ghoul hissed.

Dad turned. Turned back, a desperate look on his face. "Flo," he said. "RUN! You must run!"

But I couldn't. I just couldn't move.

Then the ghoul looked at me. Licked its lips. Bared its teeth. Took one step forward on its huge ghoul legs. One step towards me.

And the look on Dad's face changed. To fury. Total fury.

He tore the rocket out of the ground. Magic sizzled out of his spellstick and the rocket started growing. Growing and growing and growing, the touchpaper fizzing.

Then Dad charged at the ghoul, hurled himself at it, holding the rocket – the fizzing, growing rocket – like a battering ram, like a weapon.

The ghoul slashed at Dad, at the rocket, with its huge hooked Claws. Six Claws hooked into the rocket – now as big as the ghoul. Six Claws slashed through Dad's robes and hooked into his flesh.

Witchworld

The ghoul struggled and roared, and tried to get free of the rocket. Dad struggled and fought, and tried to get free of the ghoul.

And then – screeching like a creature in unbearable pain – the rocket, the giant, fizzing rocket took off.

I watched it screech upwards. Up and up, with Dad and the ghoul still struggling. Still fighting. Still hooked to the rocket, to each other, by those terrible, terrible Claws.

I watched it soar in a vast screeching arc through the sky.

I watched until it was just a tiny speck far above.

Then I watched it explode. Explode and fall – in a burst of light, of sparks, of colours and patterns and shapes in the sky – straight over the heart of the Ice Volcano.

I curled myself up in a tight tight ball on the ground. And that's where they found me.

✦

And now, right here, right now, tears – torrents of them – gushed down my face.

Because now I remembered. Now I knew.

My dad . . . my lovely, lovely dad was gone. No more playing. No more laughing. No more anything. No more Dad ever EVER again.

And here, now, Hetty. I couldn't save her. Not Hetty, not the witchteens, not any of them.

I couldn't save myself.

Because the ghoul took a step towards me.

It licked its terrible lips. It bared its terrible teeth.

And it stretched out its Claws, its *terrible* Claws.

Chapter 38

GRATED DRAGON'S TOOTH

DRIED TROLL TOENAILS

No. NO. Something changed in my head. In *me*.

Right there, right then – as that towering monster stretched out its Claws...

A feeling surged through me. A feeling of *fury*.

Fury at the ghoul who took Dad. At the ghouls snarling and hissing and circling inside Hurlstruk House.

Fury at THIS ghoul.

Fury that surged and fizzed right through me. Fury that made me feel strong, powerful, like I had the strength of three, five – *ten* witchkids. Made me feel I could climb buildings, leap mountains. Do things I never normally could.

And I knew. This ghoul – this stinking ugly brute of a ghoul – was *not* going stop me saving Hetty. It was NOT.

Thud. The ghoul took one step nearer.

Its eyes gleamed. It grinned. It licked its lips. Then it waited. Waited for me to run.

Well, I *wasn't* running. I was not running anywhere.

No chance – that's what Grandma said witchkids had. No chance against a rogue ghoul. But maybe Grandma was WRONG. Maybe there *was* something a witchkid could use against a towering ghoul like this one.

Like brains. And cunning.

So I stood right where I was. Right where I wanted to be. In the doorway of Hurlstruk House.

Because behind me – through the doorway – ghouls were leaping, snarling, circling. But witchteens were fighting. Shrieking and screaming – but fighting. *Still* fighting.

"Come and get me!" I hissed.

The ghoul hunched. The ghoul crouched. It got ready to spring.

Spikes – I could see spikes. Strong spikes running up its huge spiny back. Spikes up to its shoulders.

Spikes up to its neck. Like a ladder…

With a snarl the ghoul sprang — but I was ready. Did the Run-for-it Roll, then scrambled away. Ran behind it.

I grabbed hold of one spike, of two — and I started to climb.

The feel of that skin, scaly and rotten. . . The icy-cold touch of those spikes on my arms. . . The smell of that flesh, the choking on ghoul breath, the snarls and the growls, and the sounds in my ears…

I'll NEVER forget it.

But thoughts of Dad, thoughts of Hetty, thoughts of those snarling, circling ghouls swirled through my brain.

And still that fury surged through me — so strong, so powerful. Giving strength to my arms, to my legs, to every bit of me.

So I climbed and I climbed. Up that three-metre ghoul, that giant, that *monster*. Up those spikes, cold as ice blocks. Past huge, spiny wings. Right up to its shoulders.

Then I stood on a spike. Clamped an arm round its strong ghoul neck. And I got out the wand.

The ghoul raged. It tossed its head, gnashed its teeth, tried to reach up and grab me. It lunged, and it bucked, and it reared, and it grabbed. It howled, and it roared, and it snarled, and it raged – but it could NOT reach me.

I gripped the wand, with one freezing hand. I had to do the spell. Keep Hetty safe. HAD to. But I was cold. *So* cold. Words stumbled from my mouth through my chattering teeth.

"Abrakkida Mutattikk, Puelliki Intrik," I said. "Diversikka, Optikka, Lune."

And still the ghoul bucked, still the ghoul roared. Thrashed its arms. Thrashed its head.

And still I clung on.

I would do the spell. I would keep Hetty safe. I WOULD. But … my hands – I couldn't feel them. Not any more. And my mouth – it was numb. Almost too numb to speak. But I had to. *Had* to.

"Parvik Non, Mordik Non…" I said. "Revikkto Zin Rovvik…"

I could hardly hold on. Hardly keep a grip. Hardly speak.

Then I saw her. Hetty…

Hetty – with a ghoul towering over her. Baring huge sharp teeth. *Hetty!* No. NO.

Memories flashed through my head, one after another after another.

Hetty showing me how to hold a spellstick. Hetty holding my hand as I walked along a wall. Hetty

240

telling me pixie stories when I was sick. Hetty helping me with Potions homework. Hetty giving me a leg-up on my first unicorn ride.

"Aggesida! Elkida! Ferune!" I shouted, through chattering teeth.

Then, with one frozen hand, I pointed the wand – and it glowed. Bright as fire. A shower of stardust, burst after burst after burst, swirled out of the wand. Swirled in through the doorway – as the ghoul threw me off, and I crashed to the ground.

I staggered to my feet. So cold, so icy *icy* cold, I could hardly think. Hardly move. But I had to. *Had* to.

Because there was still one thing – one thing I HAD to do.

So I staggered and stumbled to the huge glass doors of Hurlstruk House. Dragged them tight shut.

And I locked them.

Then I turned. And I *cowered*...

Chapter 39

The ghoul took a step — one monstrous step — towards me. Snarling with fury. Baring its teeth, its black, stinking teeth.

I pressed myself back against the huge glass doors.

Howls were coming from inside. Howl after howl after howl. Howls of fear? Or of pleasure? I just didn't know.

But one thing I *did* know.

Whichever they were — Skritchetts had failed. Skritchetts would NOT save Witchworld.

Because Mum was not here. And with no Mum, no witches, there was no hope. No way to stop the ghoul attack.

So I cowered – alone.

All alone.

With a rogue ghoul, three times my size, towering above me. A ghoul stretching out its Claws. Its terrible, terrible Claws…

Except I *wasn't* alone.

Because a tiny blue streak came hurtling out of Hurlstruk House – from some hole, somewhere, somehow – whiskers bristling, tail rattling, teeth gnashing.

A nibbet.

A *furious* nibbet.

A nibbet that leapt right on to that rogue ghoul's back, scuttled up its huge spines, clamped a set of tiny pointy nibbet teeth round its monstrous left ear – and hung on.

And I knew, just knew, it was Hetty.

Hetty – and my spell. My doppel spell. A spell to keep the witchteens safe, to make them look like nibbets. Not nibbets good enough to fool other nibbets, but nibbets good enough to fool ghouls…

Even a rogue ghoul like this one.

And now there were more nibbets. Nibbets, one after another, scampering out from wherever that nibbet hole – that brilliant, wonderful nibbet hole – was. An army of nibbets. Witchteen nibbets, who leapt, gnashing and bristling, straight at that monstrous ghoul.

And the rogue ghoul was howling. Cowering and dodging. With room for one thought only in its ugly ghoul head.

Panic.

But then – I heard something. Loud thudding, loud thumping. The loud thudding and thumping of ghouls battering their way out of Hurlstruk House. Battering their way out through the doors.

Then those doors, those huge glass doors, began to crack. Began to splinter. And – KERRANG! – they shattered into tiny pieces.

Howls filled the air. The howls of ghouls about to break free.

"Nooooo!" I heard myself yelling. "NOOOOOOOO!" After all this – after all we had done – the ghouls were free. Free to swarm, to move on, free to attack any witches in their way.

Like the witchboys from Gargoyles, coming in for a landing.

The ghouls didn't get the chance.

From way up in the sky – that big black sky –

244

came a roaring sound, louder and louder and louder.

The roar of skyriders. Thousands of skyriders. Thousands and *thousands* of skyriders.

Skyriders streaming across the sky. Skyriders streaming towards Harridan's, towards us. Skyriders stretched out sideways as far as my eyes could see.

An army of *Hocus Pocus* readers. Rows and rows and rows of them in lines across the sky. Flexipods open, spellsticks at the ready – and a ferocious look on every face.

And, right at the front, Mum. And Grandma. With the most ferocious look of all. The ferocious look of Skritchetts about to save Witchworld.

And they did.

Mum, Grandma and the army of *Hocus Pocus* readers.

The first ghouls flew out through the splintered glass door – and the power of magic from thousands and thousands of spellsticks surged towards them.

And I watched as those spellsticks, those thousands of spellsticks, froze every ghoul as it flew.

I watched as icicles formed, as the ghouls dribbled and raged, and struggled to flap their huge, spiny wings.

I watched as – slowly, slowly, slowly – the shrieking

and howling and struggling faded away.

And then the ghouls were silent. Frozen and twisted. Forming terrifying shapes in the sky. Shapes with snarling mouths, stretched-out arms, flapping wings and staring eyes.

Monstrous statues of cold white ice. The icy white shapes of my Shudders.

And – most monstrous of all – the rogue ghoul.

Frozen as the nibbets scampered off its back. Frozen as it leapt towards me. Frozen in mid-roar. Frozen with its Claws – its terrible, terrible Claws – reaching out to grab me.

Frozen – just like the others – for ever.

Part
Five

Chapter 40

The government did something useful for once. The First Witchminister sent a fleet of refrigeration skytrucks to Hurlstruk House. The ghouls were loaded on – one to each truck – then the trucks set off, heading north to the Frozen Wastes.

And that was it. The ghouls were gone. Doomed to be snarling, twisted statues of ice for ever.

While out in the Harridan's gardens, thousands and thousands of witches – witchteens, witchteachers, witchministers, witchhacks, witchscreen crews and *Hocus Pocus* readers – all threw handbags and hats and briefcases in the air, all grabbed and twirled and danced each other around, all whooping and cheering and cheering.

Only me and Mum and Hetty stood, in a small sad group. Not cheering, not whooping, not dancing. Not doing anything. Just thinking of Dad.

"He was a hero," Mum sniffed. "The bravest of witchmen."

"He saved you, and he saved Witchworld, Flo," Hetty said, pale and miserable. "We should be really, really glad about that." Then she put her head on my shoulder and started howling.

"Now Flo has remembered," said Mum, dabbing her eyes. "We can all be at peace."

Grandma just snorted. "Kristabel," she said. "Stop talking nonsense."

Then she turned to Hetty. "Hetty," said Grandma. "Are you at peace?"

"Yes, Grandma," Hetty howled. "At least we know. At least we don't have to wonder what happened. Not any more. I am totally at peace, thank you."

"Well, you don't sound as if you are," said Grandma.

Then she turned to me. "Flo," she said. "Are you at peace?"

"I'm not exactly sure what at peace means, Grandma," I said, sniffing. "If at peace means sad lurching feelings inside then, yes, I'm at peace."

And I couldn't help it: I gave a big sniff. "But knowing how Dad died doesn't make me feel better," I said. "Not one bit."

"Died?" said Grandma, looking astonished and handing me her hanky. "It would take more than a rocket and a ghoul and an Ice Volcano to make Lyle Skritchett dead."

Mum went dark green. "Mother," she said. "This is irresponsible. You are giving false hope to young witches who need closure."

"Kristabel," said Grandma. "I have absolutely no idea what you're talking about. What on earth is closure? And why do Hetty and Flo need it?"

"They must accept he's gone. That he had no chance against the ghoul!" Mum hissed. "They must grieve over their loss. Then they can move on, remember the happy times!"

Grandma was looking more and more astonished. "Really, Kristabel, this is Lyle Skritchett we're talking about. Lyle Skritchett, who wrestled a seven-horned truggerdon and won. Lyle Skritchett, champion harpy hurdler."

Then she tutted. "You were married to him, Kristabel. You really should know him much better than this. And, Kristabel, I never did say this – but he was far too good for you. Silliest mistake you ever made losing him."

"I did NOT lose him, Mother. We *divorced*," hissed Mum through gritted teeth.

"And I'm not surprised," said Grandma severely. "You'll have to work very hard to win him back when he returns. Still – at least you're older now. Not quite as silly as you were. You may have a chance."

"Win him back?" screeched Mum, slapping her head.

"It's always possible," said Grandma. "After all, he kept your name. Never changed it back."

Then Grandma grinned her big gappy grin at me, and at Hetty. "Your father can handle a ghoul and a rocket and the Ice Volcano," she said confidently. "He'll be back."

Hetty looked at me. She scratched her head. "Totally not sure what to think here, Flo," she said. "Help me out. You're brainy. You always know the answer."

And I did.

"Hetty," I said. And a great big beam was spreading right across my face – and I couldn't stop it, and I didn't want to. "I *do* know the answer. And it's this. That Grandma is *right*."

Witchworld

Because Grandma – my stubborn, grumpy, impossible Grandma – of course she was right. She *was*.

Chapter 41

So that's it. The story of the ghoul attack in South Witchenland. So all you witchkids know what to look out for.

Because Grandma says if one ghoul broke out in Witchenwild, and lots of ghouls broke out in Haggspit – then any number of ghouls could break out anywhere.

Which is why Grandma is now Government Adviser on Ghouls. She's got a whole government department checking for ghouls twenty-four hours a day – and every single witchminister is terrified of her. She says she missed the signs of ghouls with

Dad and she is NOT missing them again.

She's got a government desk, government ID and she's got her own office in Argument House.

But – and I probably shouldn't tell you this, but I'm hoping the government are too busy with meetings to read a book written for witchkids – she still hasn't let on about her magic mirror.

Oh no.

Not Grandma.

As for Mum, she *did* get all my calls and webmails. And two hours after the ghoul attack ended, I got a webmail too – from Babblechat:

```
APOLOGIES FOR CALL AND WEBMAIL
            PROBLEMS.
        SYSTEM FAULT.
    REPAIRS NOW COMPLETE.
```

Then my skychatter beeped again. Twenty-eight times. Because I had fourteen delayed calls and fourteen delayed webmails. All from Mum, of course.

Me and Hetty – we should have realised. We were so busy thinking about how we could NOT get hold of Mum, that we forgot to think about something else…

Maybe it was Mum who could NOT get hold of us.

Because Hetty was right. Mum *did* check her skychatter in the very first break. She tried to call me, but no incoming calls or webmails were getting through on Babblechat. And, later – no outgoing ones either.

After the ghoul attack was over, the big bosses who publish *Hocus Pocus* had a meeting about Mum. Discussed what to do. Seems they had trouble deciding if she was hero or villain.

Because Mum did a LOT of lying to her readers. When she got my first message, she abandoned Conference and got busy on the witchweb. With this:

HURRY! HURRY! HURRY!
EXTRAS WANTED!
RIVALS **FILMING TONIGHT!**
MEET MICKY RATIZZO!

She offered her readers the chance of a lifetime.

She said *Rivals* was filming a special at Harridan's and needed *Hocus Pocus* readers – thousands of them – to be extras.

She said that the *Rivals* special was all about what might happen if ghouls were actually real.

She said the extras' job – led by her – was to stream towards Harridans in their groups, looking ferocious, then do the freezing spell on the ghouls.

She said to turn up for rehearsals right away at the airstrip belonging to HighFlyers – which is the skycab company Mum uses.

She said every witch who turned up for rehearsals would get to meet Micky Ratizzo that night. And that one lucky reader would win a meal in Haggspit Harbour's finest diner with him.

More than *four thousand seven hundred* witches turned up.

Mum spent hours training them all up. And Grandma helped too – because when Grandma woke and read my note, she called Mum and joined her.

Then the two of them got busy. Sorting witches into groups, into rows, stacking them up in the sky, drilling them so no witch would get in the way of magic streaming from another witch's spellstick, getting them to practise the freezing spell over and over again.

So the big bosses of *Hocus Pocus* spent four hours in their meeting, arguing about whether Mum was a hero or a villain. In the end, they set up a voting line and got the readers to decide.

The readers voted Mum a hero. One hundred per cent of them.

Mum ran a thirty-eight-page special about the ghoul attack. Starting with the cover – a picture of Mum, and Grandma, and the *Hocus Pocus* readers outside Hurlstruk House, all cheering, with frozen ghouls behind them, being loaded into skytrucks, and a headline:

WE DID IT, GIRLS!

And it included a VERY big feature on Grandma – because Grandma really made Mum suffer for thinking she had Confusions.

"Grovel, Kristabel," she said. "GROVEL. Apologise. Admit that the only Skritchett with ANY kind of Confusions was *you*."

So Mum grovelled. Mum apologised. And then Mum got Grandma's room redecorated.

Because Grandma's still living with us. Still brewing up potions. Still driving Mum nuts.

And Grandma did some grovelling too. To her wand. The small stubby wand. She even bought a special lined case to keep it in, with soft sides, so if it jiggles a lot it doesn't hurt itself.

Hetty was in *Hocus Pocus* too, along with all the other witchteens. On the fashion pages. Modelling old-style robes – loose, and in shades of black and grey – all holding wands and wearing pointy hats.

Retro chic, Mum called it.

All the witchteens are wearing retro chic at the moment. It won't last though – fashion never does.

And when the circulation figures for that issue came out, Mum couldn't stop beaming. "Up by sixty-two per cent," she said happily. "Biggest scoop of my career!"

★

As for Hetty, did the ghoul attack change her? Did she realise she had great strengths, great qualities, great leadership skills? Did she realise that there were more important things in life than getting a boyfriend, or a nose job, or being famous?

No.

First, because she actually IS quite famous. Right now, anyway. And believe me, she's making the most of it.

Second, because the Prom – the actual Prom, a Prom with no ghouls this time – is being held this Saturday. And any time I knock on Hetty's door she tells me to go away and find some big creepy ghoul to fight, because she's busy with her list of things to do.

I sneaked a look at it.

```
Develop tinkling cackle

Learn names of all players in Premier League
  gripball teams

Practise wiggly walk

Update image file of possible noses
```

Which leaves me.

First, Harridan's. They've changed their minds about me. They've offered me a place because I saved their witchteens. In fact, they've offered me a scholarship.

Second, the government. The government gave me some prize money for my part in the ghoul attack. I used it to buy another fake Freefall Forest tree for the pixies.

I go and see them quite a lot – but Plucky's not there any more. I reckon he got bored with being a pixie. Made a break for it. Squirmed out through the netting one hour he was in his maggot shape.

But without Plucky, without taking the doppel potion, I'd never have known that ghouls were scared of nibbets. That a doppel spell would keep the witchteens safe.

And without knowing that, things might have turned out quite differently. For Hetty, for the witchteens – and for me.

So good luck to him, I say. Wherever he is…

Third, explanations. Grandma still owes me some explanations. About Great-Grandma, and the day she got her Shudders. About the Blob, and why she's so sure the Deadly Dodger Attack is true, not a myth.

I keep telling her she owes me – but you can NOT rush Grandma. And I know she *will* tell me… I just don't know when. But that's Grandma for you.

As for my Shudders, I'm hoping that was the one and only Shudder I ever have. Really hoping. Because I don't want to see the future. No one should.

And, so far, that IS my one and only Shudder. But who knows…

Fourth, headlines. Mum wanted me to be a big story spread across pages 5-7. She wanted a big headline at the top, and lots of pictures.

I said no. I said Mum could tell my story, my part in the ghoul attack. But only one page, and one small picture. And NO big headline.

Lily and Kika were cross with me. They kept flapping page 48 of the Book in my face, and saying I should be practising my celebrity signature and working on my celebrity wave, instead of refusing to have a big story with a big headline.

But I've had enough of being headlines. Especially these sort of headlines:

TRAGIC FLO REMEMBERS DAD'S DEATH
TRAGIC FLO AT PEACE NOW

That's the sort of thing the headlines all say. That I can be at peace, remembering how Dad died, knowing that he died to save me from a ghoul attack.

Well, they're wrong, and Grandma is right.

Because Dad made me a promise. "The Seven Wonders of Witchworld," he said. "One day we'll see them all – I promise."

And now there's one more. An Eighth Wonder of Witchworld.

The Ice Statues of the Frozen Wastes.

Witchworld

The ghouls.

There was a ceremony, and me and Grandma were special guests. And I stood there in the Frozen Wastes listening to long boring speeches, with snow falling all round me – wishing and wishing that Dad was there with me.

He will be one day.

Yes. One day me and Dad will see all Eight Wonders of Witchworld. I *know* we will.

One day.